praise for *These* [barcode: D0864127]

The crafted stories of Jyotsna Sr _____ ____
Americans *offer the perspectives* _____*grant and native-born Indian Americans as they balance Indian culture with the expectations of American life. . . . Though there are subtle variations in tone and setting, the stories of These Americans form a cohesive, captivating collection.*

— Foreword Reviews

The stories are a valuable addition to the more complex panorama of American life that readers are, at last, eager to read.
— *Breena Clarke, author of* River, Cross My Heart *(Oprah book club selection) and* Stand the Storm *(named one of the 100 best books of 2008 by the Washington Post)*

A quietly tender—and occasionally hilarious—meditation on life, family, and immigration.
— *Marie Myung-Ok Lee, author of* Somebody's Daughter *and a founder of the Asian American Writer's Workshop*

The stories in These Americans *explore with lightness and eloquence the complexity of living between cultures. Sreenivasan writes beautifully about childhood and about the very particular complications that women face as wives and mothers. A wonderful novella, "Hawk", completes the collection with a heartrending account of a mother and daughter navigating prejudice at home and at work. A dazzling and lovely collection.*
— *Margot Livesey, author of* Mercury *and* The Hidden Machinery

These Americans

These Americans

short stories and a novella

by

Jyotsna Sreenivasan

MINERVA RISING
PRESS

Tampa

ISBN 978-1-950811-06-9

Cover Art by Lauren Chidel
Book design by Brooke Schultz

Printed and bound in USA
First Printing May 2021

Published by Minerva Rising Press
9501 Bessie Coleman Blvd #21802
Tampa, FL 33622-1082
www.minervarising.com

contents

MIRROR

I'm lying on this hard hospital delivery bed with only a small thin robe over my body. My legs, even my knees, are all uncovered, and my bare feet are in these stirrups. It's indecent, how you must be to give birth. In India do they cover the women more? I don't know, but here in America, no one cares, they go about in shorts and swimming suits anyway, even the old fat ladies do it, exposing all their white wrinkled flesh just like that.

My hands and arms are cold. My stomach is a big mountain. Every so often it gets hard and I know I'm having a contraction. It doesn't hurt at all. They gave me a shot in my back. It is called an epidural. I'm glad. I was afraid I would scream and embarrass myself.

The American nurse comes in. She's thin and tall. She wears a short white skirt and white stockings and white shoes and a white cap. She smiles. I have gotten used to these Americans smiling all the time. When I first came here in April of

1965, almost two years ago, I thought, why are they always laughing at me? At first, I thought, it's my sari and my kumkum. They have never seen someone wearing a sari and kumkum before. Then, after I took off the kumkum and began wearing skirts and shaving my legs and everything, still they laughed. I thought, what's wrong with me, that they should be showing their teeth every time I appear? Maybe it's because I'm brown, I thought. But they have seen brown people before. There are plenty of these Africans everywhere, Negroes they call them, and they would also laugh at me. I could not understand it. Finally, I asked my friend Betty Pryor. She's my closest friend in America. She is a single lady and she owns a house and we stay in the apartment in the basement. Imagine, a single lady owning her own house and even renting it to strangers!

Betty told me, "Prema, they are not laughing at you. They are just being friendly. You must also smile when you meet someone." Then she said, "You have a beautiful smile."

No one ever told me I was beautiful before. The next morning, after I brushed my teeth, I looked at myself in the bathroom mirror. A frowning brown lady was there staring at me. I opened my lips and stretched them into a smile. The lady in the mirror looked funny, and I began laughing. And there was a pretty lady laughing back at me. Then I felt ashamed of myself and left the bathroom. Who did I think I was? A princess or something?

My husband isn't here yet. He's a resident doctor at this hospital and that's why he will be allowed to be with me at the birth. He's just finishing up some work and he'll be here soon. Otherwise, I would have to be all alone. I'm glad I will not be all alone.

In India, I would have my baby in the "nursing home" near my mother's house. That's what they call the places where ladies go to have babies—nursing homes. The place is just two streets from my mother's house. It's in the home of a doctor—a lady doctor, of course. In India, they don't have men doctors for ladies. But here they think nothing of having a man look at that part of a lady and put his fingers in and everything. It's disgusting. But what to do? Here I am in America.

My elder sister went to the nursing home last year to have her baby and I still have not seen my first niece. I don't know when we will go back home. Sometimes I wonder, why did I agree to marry a man who wanted to study in America? I thought it would be fun to come here. I saw pictures of American homes in magazines, and everything looked so nice, so clean. When I was a little girl, I thought people in America must not ever use the toilet. I could not imagine such large white people ever needing to do something dirty like that. It's funny what children think about.

"How're we doing, Mrs.—" The nurse looks at a piece of paper on a clipboard. "How d'you say your name?"

"Mrs. Sridhar," I say. "I am fine, thank you." I smile a little bit. I am too cold to smile very much.

The nurse pushes up my robe and puts her fingers in down there. This is the part I hate about having a baby, having everyone feeling around down there. "Good," she says. "Eight centimeters. When you start pushing, I can adjust this mirror so you can see." She points to a round mirror above the bed.

"See what?"

"So you can see the baby coming out!" she exclaims.

"Oh. No. No." Then I remember my manners. "No, thank you." Only in America would they have something so the woman can see! What is there to see? It's bad enough to have all this happening down there, in that part of my body. But what can I do? God made us give birth from there. Don't ask me why. Seeing isn't going to help anything.

The nurse leaves the room. I don't know where my husband is. At the time I agreed to come to America, I had no idea what it would really be like. When I first arrived here, there were no leaves at all on the trees. I thought, so America is like this, with no leaves on the trees, no flowers. I have come from India, which is full of flowers, to this God-forsaken place. I was so unhappy. Before I arrived I thought, my husband is a doctor, and we will be going to the richest country in the world. I will live like a queen. I didn't know the hospital did not pay residents well. I didn't know we would have to live in a basement apartment with paint and everything falling off the ceiling. I didn't know we would not be able to find basic Indian groceries, not even dal or ghee or yogurt. At home we have a cook and I never learned to make my own ghee or yogurt. Here I somehow make something or other using split peas and corn oil and sour cream. My mother sends me spices every so often, sambar powder and rasam powder, but I cannot find fresh chillies or coriander leaves. The only coconut in the store here is dried and sweetened, so I cannot use it. Imagine, eating South Indian food without coriander leaves or coconut!

But it's not so bad. I am used to it now. The main thing was, I was bored. My husband was at the hospital all day and even at night sometimes. I have learned to drive, but where could I go? There is only one other Indian couple near us, and both of them, husband and wife, are doctors, so they are both just as busy. How to spend my time? Besides cooking and cleaning, I did some knitting and I went upstairs to watch TV with Betty. Finally, one day I said to my husband, let's have a baby. My mother is writing asking why we are not expecting yet. I need some way to spend my time. Let's have a baby.

So here I am in the hospital. The nurse comes in again and checks me. "Ten centimeters," she says. "You're ready." The doctor is here now, a man doctor. He's wearing a mask and is pulling on some rubber gloves.

The nurse puts her hand on my stomach. "OK, push now," she says. So, every time I feel my stomach tighten, I push as hard as I can.

"Good!" the nurse says. "I can see the head. Are you sure you don't want to see?"

I put my elbows on the bed and try to sit up. I want to see my baby.

"Lie down," she says. "You can't see that way. You need to use the mirror."

"Yes," I say. "Yes, I want to see." My heart is going thump-thump-thump so fast.

The nurse pulls the mirror down and I can see a shiny black-haired head. I can see what the man doctor is seeing. I don't care that he is looking at that part of me. I want to see my baby's face.

"Push," the nurse says.

I hold my breath and push. The head comes out. The face is turned the other way.

"Good," says the doctor. "Push again."

I see the rest of the body slide out, and the doctor catches it. "It's a girl!" he says.

A girl. I wanted a boy first, and then a girl next. I wanted a big brother who would protect his younger sister. But I have a girl! I thank God. Anyway, my older brother never protected me. A girl is good. I hold out my arms.

The nurse laughs. "So, you wanted to see after all. I'll clean her off."

I don't want to wait. Just then my husband arrives. I had forgotten about him. "A girl!" I shout to him. "There she is."

He peeks over the nurse's shoulder. I'm jealous that he gets to see her first, when I'm the one who's been carrying her. "Bring her here," I say.

He brings her to me all wrapped up tight in a white blanket. Only her face shows. I try to sit up and take her, but the doctor, who's still doing something down there, says, "Lie still!"

So, I can only look. Her black eyes stare at me. "She's so white!" I exclaim. "Why is she so white?" I wonder if this is one more thing I didn't know about America—that babies born here turn white.

"It's OK," my husband says. "Even Indian babies are white when they're first born."

I look at her dark eyes and dark hair. I touch her cheek with one finger, and she turns her mouth towards my finger. "She thinks it is food!" I say.

Even while I am still lying down, I put on a big smile. I have a beautiful smile. I am not the ignorant girl who came from India in the winter, who didn't even know about springtime in Ohio. I am a mother now.

My baby starts shrieking. She has good lungs. "What, are you my American child?" I ask. "I saw you come out in that round mirror," I tell her. "Here in America, they have things like that, so Amma can see her princess right away."

AT HOME

Summer, 1974

Amiya looked out the kitchen window. There was a play-ground next to their new townhouse: swing-set, metal slide, and monkey bars, with sand all around. Next to that, a square of black paving with a bottomless basket on top of a tall pole. She wondered what that was for. Behind her, at the rented kitchen table, her mother drank coffee with Mrs. Kaminski.

"I did not think we would have to come back to America," her mother said.

Amiya was bored with this statement. Mommy had been saying it for months, ever since they'd decided to move back to the US.

"We went there with the idea of settling down," her mother said. "Somehow it was not meant to be."

"You'll get settled here soon," Mrs. Kaminski soothed.

"I thought I would finally have my mother's help in raising the children. I never thought I would have to raise children in this country, away from everyone."

Amiya was always amazed that her mother still needed *her* mother. She had seen her grandmother for the first time two years ago, at the Bangalore airport. Her grandmother was a short, fat woman in a sari. Every morning her grandmother oiled her graying hair with coconut oil. At the airport on the way here, her grandmother had clung to her and said in Kannada, "Don't forget us."

"Go outside and play, Amiya," Mommy said.

"I am waiting for Vinod," Amiya said. Her father and brother had gone to look at a used car advertised for sale.

"She talks just like an Indian," Mrs. Kaminski remarked. "I can't believe she's seven already. When you left, she still had those fat cheeks, and now she's so tall and thin! Are you glad to be back, Amiya?"

Amiya remembered Mrs. Kaminski from before they left for India, two years ago. Mrs. Kaminski had a new hairstyle now, poofy and short, frosted with gold. Mrs. Kaminski's hair used to be long, straight, and dark brown. Amiya liked that style better.

Mrs. Kaminski had three children, all older than Vinod and Amiya, and this morning she had brought over two grocery bags full of old clothes for Amiya and her brother. Amiya was wearing a pair of sky-blue shorts and a striped red shirt from those bags.

"Mrs. Kaminski is asking you a question, Amiya," her mother reminded her.

Amiya looked down at her bare toes. "Yes," she mumbled. In India, everyone had asked whether she was sad to go. Here, they asked if she was glad to be back. In India, her aunties and grandmother had cried. Here, Mrs. Kaminski welcomed them with cookies and clothes and kitchen equipment. What was there to cry about, or to be glad about? They'd moved, and she was here. She was with her parents and brother.

Mrs. Kaminski laughed. "You've grown quiet," she said. "You used to be so talkative. Your mother and I couldn't get a word in edgewise."

Amiya's mother picked up the coffee cups and set them on the counter beside the sink. "My husband says both kids have forgotten their good English, and have picked up bad Kannada."

"She'll pick up American English again soon enough," Mrs. Kaminski said, "when school starts."

Amiya was bewildered by everyone's insistence that her language had changed. She talked exactly the same way as she had before they left for India.

*

A little creek ran behind the playground. Amiya and Vinod squatted among the weeds and gazed at the dark water. Another boy, Christopher, was on the other side of the tiny creek, poking at the water with a stick.

"You can get crawdads here," Christopher said. "They pinch, though." He raised his stick. Clinging to the end of it was a tiny lobster-like creature with round bead eyes and hairy tentacles waving. Christopher shoved it at Amiya's face. "Nyaaah!"

She flinched, and Christopher screeched with laughter.

"Don't scare my sister," Vinod threatened.

Amiya reached for Christopher's stick and examined the helpless little creature dangling in the air. She never saw crawdads in India. She never played in a creek in India. They'd lived in the middle of a city. Her grandfather took her to see the afternoon train rumble by on the tracks near their house. She had once played in a gravel pile left by some construction workers.

Before they'd moved to India, they had also lived in a city: Cleveland. Mommy used to walk her and Vinod to the playground shaded by big trees.

She dipped the stick back in the water and the crawdad, feeling the earth, let go.

"Hey!" Christopher shouted. "Now I gotta catch it again! I wanna put it in my aquarium."

Amiya sat back on her heels. Christopher reminded her of Vinod's friend Mohan in India. Mohan was also like this, trying to scare her, pretending he knew everything.

"It will not like to be kept in an aquarium," she said.

Christopher wrinkled his brow at her. "How come you talk so funny?"

*

On the other side of the street, Amiya saw two girls sitting on the sidewalk. She crossed and stood next to them. One girl had long hair, like Amiya's friend Nandika in India. The other girl had short hair, like Bindu.

"What are you doing?" Amiya asked.

The girls looked up at her. They both had their legs spread, bare soles of feet touching, and in the space made by their legs Amiya saw a small red ball and several strange cross-shaped things, like two X's put together.

"Whadja say?" the girl with the long hair asked.

"What are you doing?" Amiya repeated.

Both girls turned back to the objects on the ground. The short-haired girl flung the ball against the ground and, while it bounced high in the air, made a grab for the cross-shaped things. The ball hit the ground outside their legs and rolled away under a bush.

Amiya retrieved the ball and gave it back to the short-haired girl, who slit her eyes at Amiya when she accepted it.

"What is your name?" Amiya asked.

"Wha'?" The short-haired girl squinted up at her.

"Your name," Amiya repeated.

"Oh. Um. Cheryl."

"My name is Amiya."

"Oh."

The long-haired girl didn't say anything. Cheryl said, "That's Julie."

"I'm going in," Julie said. "It's too hot." She jumped up, ran to the nearest door, and slammed it behind her.

Cheryl stood up slowly, keeping her eyes on Amiya.

"Will you come to my home?" Amiya asked.

"What?"

"Will you come home? To play."

Cheryl shrugged. "OK." She leaned down, scooped up the cross-shaped things, and stuffed them into the pocket of her shorts.

Amiya led the way across the street. Inside, the house was dim and cool. Cheryl stood on the carpet in her bare feet. "Where's your furniture?"

"Right here." Amiya pointed to the sofa.

"That's it?"

"We just moved here."

"Didn't you bring furniture from where you came from?"

Amiya shook her head. "It was too far."

Cheryl scratched a mosquito bite on her leg and looked around the empty room. Amiya's heart was clutched by panic: she had almost no toys to show Cheryl. She'd left her American toys—her puzzles and plastic animals and nice Barbie in its plastic carrying case, with clothes made by her mother—she'd left them all in India, for her cousins to play with. Now she had a stuffed kitten and a watercolor set, which her parents bought for her a few days after they had arrived. She also had some toys Mrs. Kaminski had brought over: a couple of dirty Barbie dolls with a few stained outfits, and a game called Tiddlywinks.

Cheryl didn't want to play Tiddlywinks or paint with watercolors, so Amiya brought out the Barbies. Cheryl took hers to the corner of the bedroom and, with her back to Amiya, dressed the doll and made her walk around.

Fall

On the first day of school, Amiya felt like an elephant. They'd put her back in the first grade. She didn't know why. She towered above the other first graders. When the teacher asked them to write their names at the top of a piece of paper, she wrote "Amiya" neatly in cursive. She hoped they would realize she wasn't a first grader.

The next day, a woman with short gray curls called Amiya out of her first-grade classroom and, in the hallway, showed her pictures and asked her a lot of questions.

That evening, as soon as he came in the door with his briefcase, Daddy declared, "They said Amiya should be in third grade. And Vinod should be in fifth."

Her mother stood in front of the stove, holding a roti over the bare burner. "Why did they put them in the wrong grades to begin with?" The roti puffed up and she tossed it into a round stainless steel box to keep it warm.

"They thought, since we came from India, the kids would not know as much."

"What did you say?"

"I said, just put them in second and fourth grades, where they belong."

Amiya liked being in second grade. She was the right size.

Her teacher, Miss Ferdinand, had short brown hair and red lips. On Amiya's first day in second grade, Miss Ferdinand gave everyone pieces of paper with writing on them. She asked the class to read the questions and put a checkmark beside the correct answer.

A checkmark? Amiya knew what a "check" was: a little square. She drew a neat square beside each correct answer.

Miss Ferdinand stopped beside Amiya's desk. She smelled like lipstick. Miss Ferdinand put out a white hand, with long pink nails, and slid Amiya's yellow pencil out of her fist. She wrote a dark V, with one tail longer, beside Amiya's checks. "That is a checkmark," Miss Ferdinand explained.

There was one very pretty girl in the class: Jessie Lombardi. She had shiny dark-gold hair and dimples. She looked like a princess. On the playground, Jessie threw up her hands, lifted a knee, hopped, and fell onto her palms. But she didn't actually fall. She spun, her legs apart and straight, and landed on her feet. She did it again. And again. Amiya grew dizzy watching. All the other girls did it too, but Jessie was the best. Amiya tried: she threw up her hands, raised her knee, cautiously put her hands down and hopped with her feet.

Jessie laughed. "That's not a cartwheel."

A cartwheel. Amiya wanted to do that. Every day at recess she practiced with the other girls, and before the weather turned cold, she could do a perfect cartwheel, her legs spinning straight in the air.

*

Jessie had a birthday party in October. Amiya bought her a stuffed kitten just like her own. But she didn't have a pretty party dress to wear. "You can wear a langa," Mommy said.

Jessie's living room was warm and bright when Amiya

stepped inside, wearing her pink and gold floor-length silk skirt and her lumpy wrapped gift.

"What a beautiful outfit!" Jessie's mother exclaimed.

"Thank you," Amiya said politely.

Jessie walked into the living room. She wore a blue and white dress with satin roses, and a blue headband. Amiya gave her the present and Jessie said, "That's my grandmother." Amiya saw a black-haired woman wearing a skirt that showed her knees and legs, sitting in a chair. The tops of her feet bulged out of her shoes, as if they had been stuffed into them.

"Let's sit here to wait for everyone else," Jessie said, and they both sat down on the sofa. The grandmother smiled at them. "Your skirt is just gorgeous," she said to Amiya.

Amiya stood up and twirled around, making the long skirt balloon out. The grandmother exclaimed. Amiya squatted down suddenly in the middle of the balloon. This was a trick you could do with a langa, but not with a dress.

"Beautiful!" The grandmother clapped.

Amiya jumped up and twirled again. She squatted down in the langa balloon again. The grandmother clapped again. "Just lovely."

Jessie stood up. "I don't think it's very pretty." She turned and marched out of the room.

Amiya, still squatting on the ground, watched her disappear. She stood up slowly, not looking at the grandmother, and sank onto the sofa.

*

Amiya's mother rustled around the kitchen in a silk sari. Her lips were red today, like Miss Ferdinand's. She smelled like the perfume in the tiny crystal bottle she kept on her dresser.

They were having a Deepavali party. Amiya had been

allowed to wear one of her mother's gold necklaces, with the beautiful mango-shaped pendant set with red and white stones. The necklace rested heavily on Amiya's langa blouse.

Amiya was helping Mommy set up for the party: carrying stacks of plates to the dining table, counting out silverware. Her mother had already placed a tall brass deepa on one end of the table. Earlier in the afternoon Amiya had helped twist the cotton wicks, which were now waiting, drenched in ghee, to be lit.

"Ramu!" her mother called. She slid a tray of rice into the oven. "Ramu!"

"What?" Daddy called from upstairs

"Bring the air freshener can!" her mother shouted. She set a pot of vegetables in the oven.

"Where?" he yelled.

"In the bathroom."

Amiya's father walked in grasping a tall, thin can with flowers printed on it. Her mother took it from him and, holding the can above her head, swayed around the house. The spray hissed into the air. "Open a window," she told Amiya's father. "It smells too much like frying in here."

Amiya followed her mother, trying to catch the spray on her head as it fell. It smelled like a mixture of talcum powder and perfume.

"Everyone knows you have been frying," Daddy said. "Why should they mind the smell?" He cracked open the living room window, and a stream of cold air seeped in.

Soon the house was filled with brown faces and silk and jewelry: Pritvi and Tarun and their parents, Mythili Auntie and Pradeep Uncle; baby Nalini and her parents; a young Indian couple who both worked with her father and who were of little interest because they had no children. Mrs. Kaminski and her son Robby were also there. Mr. Kaminski never attended Indian parties because Indian food disagreed with him.

"We have sparklers!" Amiya told Pritvi. "We're gonna light them after dinner."

"She talks like an American now," Mythili Auntie commented.

"Children adapt so easily," Amiya's mother said.

"Does she still speak Kannada?" Mythili Auntie asked.

"No." Her mother slapped Amiya's head lightly. "She understands everything, but she won't speak."

"That's the way it is. Once they come here, they forget about their mother tongue."

Amiya frowned at her socks. Why did it matter how anyone talked, or what language you used?

After dinner, Mommy gave one sparkler each to Amiya, Pritvi, Tarun, Vinod, and Robby. "Let us light them in the back," her mother said. "I hope the neighbors won't notice."

"I don't know why sparklers should be illegal," Mythili Auntie said. "They are not really fireworks."

Mommy struck a match. "Hold it away from you," she warned.

When Amiya's stick hissed to life, she extended her arm as far as she could. The sparks danced out of the stick. She waved it in the dark air, watching the trails of light it left. She remembered this from India: No matter how far away you held the sparkler, one or two sparks would fall on your arm and sting.

Winter

Christmas was coming! At school, Miss Ferdinand passed out squares of thick white paper and each child drew and colored a Santa Claus. Miss Ferdinand was going to pick the ten best drawings and put them behind windows of a construction-paper house on the bulletin board. For ten days before the

Christmas holidays, Miss Ferdinand would open one window each day, and everyone would see whose drawing it was. Miss Ferdinand would put the best drawing behind the center window, which would be opened on the very last day.

Amiya knew what Santa Claus looked like. She remembered sitting on Santa's lap when she was a little girl in Cleveland. She drew her Santa Claus with a white beard, a red pointy cap, and a red coat.

After school that day, Mrs. Kaminski was sitting at the dining table drinking coffee with Amiya's mother. "I must buy some Christmas ornaments," her mother said. "I had so many nice ones, and I gave them away before we went back home."

"Back home" meant India. Amiya didn't think of India as home. Home was wherever they were.

"I did not think I would ever need them again." Her mother sighed. "Ramu says we should not bother with a tree this year. He says the kids are older. They will understand that we are not Christians."

"We're making ornaments in school," Amiya said. "Out of paper mashay." She didn't know what "mashay" meant, but she was pretty sure that's what Miss Ferdinand had said. "We covered an apple with paper mashay and when it dried Miss Ferdinand cut the ornament open and we took the apple out and glued the ornament back together with a pipe cleaner at the top for a hook, and tomorrow we're going to paint them!"

"I don't know," Amiya's mother said to Mrs. Kaminski. "Amiya is still young. And the pine tree makes the whole room smell nice. And the lights. I always like to decorate the tree."

The next day at school, Miss Ferdinand started opening the windows of the construction-paper house. The first picture was not Amiya's. It was Beth's. The picture was OK, but very faint. Beth was a pale girl who hardly ever smiled, and who never pressed hard enough with her crayons.

Every day Amiya waited with the other kids to see whose picture was next in the window. As the days went by and her picture did not appear, she started to wonder: What if her Santa wasn't there at all?

The next day Miss Ferdinand opened a window and there was Amiya's picture! Her Santa was outlined in a thick black line, and all the colors were bright. Her picture was the best so far.

But—her picture wasn't the *best*. It wasn't in the center window. Whose picture was in the center?

On the day before vacation, Miss Ferdinand opened the very center window of the house, and there was: Jessie's picture!

Jessie beamed. Amiya stared. Why was Jessie's picture better than hers?

After all the other kids went out for recess, she tugged Miss Ferdinand's sleeve. "Why is Jessie's picture better than mine?" she asked.

Miss Ferdinand swung her knees from under her desk and clicked over to the bulletin board. "Jessie's Santa is fat," Miss Ferdinand said, pointing. "Your Santa is skinny. Santa is supposed to be fat."

Miss Ferdinand was right. How could Amiya have forgotten that Santa was fat? She glared at Jessie's fat Santa, which smiled happily at everyone because it was the *best*.

*

Amiya stood in snow up to her waist, patting the snow gently with her mittens.

"I have never seen it this deep before," her mother said.

They stood in the parking lot and her father brushed off their station wagon.

"I don't know why you are bothering with that now." Mommy stood with her hands on her hips. "We are not going anywhere."

"I just want to clean it off."

"You love to clean that car. If I ask you to wash your dishes, you have no time. But for the car, you will do anything."

Amiya squatted on the sidewalk. She wanted to make a tunnel, but as she patted the snow near the ground, more from above fell down.

Vinod banged out of the house dragging his round blue saucer sled behind him. Amiya and Vinod both got sleds under the Christmas tree. Amiya also got an Easy-Bake Oven that actually baked real cakes using a lightbulb, and a Barbie Styling Head with lots of blonde hair, including a hank of hair that got longer out of the top of her head.

"It is awful." Mommy wrapped her arms around herself and surveyed the white world. "It will be like this until April. Why did we come back?"

Amiya ran into the house to get her sled. Outside, a bunch of kids were on the hill beside the row of townhouses: Vinod, Christopher, Cheryl, and Julie.

"Slide down with me, Amiya!" Cheryl called.

Amiya dragged her sled to the top of the hill and reached over to hold hands with Cheryl in her sled. Cheryl was suddenly gone, sliding down the hill, and Amiya was left at the top.

Amiya pushed against the ground with her mitten, and bumped and slipped down the hill, faster and faster. She clutched the sides of her sled. She didn't know it would be so fast.

She was at the bottom of the hill, coasting towards Cheryl.

"You were scared," Cheryl gloated.

"I was not."

"How come you had such a scared look on your face,

then?"

"I always look like that when I go sledding."

*

"Pramila Auntie sent photos!" her mother called as soon as Amiya and Vinod stepped into the house after school.

Amiya kicked off her boots and unzipped her jacket. She trotted to the dining table, trailing her scarf on the floor. Mommy held a letter in her hand, and photos were spread on the table. Amiya leaned over to look. The photos were black and white with a white border. She saw her cousin Sita wearing a langa and standing with her back to a mirror. Her braid, completely covered with white flowers, reached all the way down her back. Sita wore dangling earrings that looked like little upside-down cups, and her arms were full of bangles.

Her mother ran a finger along the braid in the photograph. "They have done moggina jade for her. A jasmine braid."

Amiya pulled at the ends of her hair. When she had first arrived in India, her hair had been short: it just covered her ears. When she saw all her cousins with long braids, she wanted to let her hair grow too. At first Mommy wouldn't let her. "You will not stand still for me to comb your hair as it is." But after a year, her mother said she could grow it out. It reached her shoulders now. She could make two short braided pigtails, but she just let it loose. No one at school wore braids.

"Look at Sita's new brother." Her mother pointed to a photo of a skinny baby lying on its back. The baby's eyes were rimmed with black kajal. There was a large round dot on its forehead.

"I just want to hold him!" her mother exclaimed. "Such a cute baby."

Amiya thought it looked kind of scary. It wasn't like the fat babies she saw on TV commercials.

Amiya left the table and rummaged in the kitchen for a Twinkie. She put the yellow cake on a plate, took it into the living room, and turned on the TV. Good. Just in time for *Marine Boy*. She loved Marine Boy, his pet dolphin Splasher, and his mermaid friend, Neptina.

"I don't know when we will see them all again." Her mother still sat at the dining table, shuffling the photos back and forth in her hands.

Amiya was glad to be in the US, where they had TV. She wished she lived in the ocean like Marine Boy. She would be Neptina, with a yellow fish tail and blue hair, and she would wear a pearl that let her see into the future.

Spring

Miss Ferdinand stood at the front of the class. She smiled and clasped her hands together in front of her chest. "I have a special announcement to make today," she said. "Our school will have an international fair next month. Every class will choose one country to learn about. And because we have someone from India in this class—" Miss Ferdinand extended her arm in Amiya's direction— "we will choose India!"

Every head in the class turned to stare at Amiya. She dropped her gaze to her desk. Her face burned. She wanted to disappear.

"What do you say, Amiya?" Miss Ferdinand coaxed.

Amiya wasn't sure what she was supposed to say. "Thank you," she mumbled to her desk.

Miss Ferdinand talked on and on, her voice raising and lowering itself, explaining about the international fair. Amiya sat as still as she could. After many long moments, she dared to raise her eyes. Most heads had turned away from her, back to Miss Ferdinand.

"And Amiya will carry the Indian flag in our parade!" Miss Ferdinand concluded. "Won't that be fun, Amiya?"

All heads swiveled back to her. Amiya's eyes returned to her desk.

*

"Your teacher called today," her mother said as they were having dinner. "She says you are not happy about the international fair." Her mother stirred the pot of sambar in the middle of the table before ladling some of it onto her father's rice.

How had Miss Ferdinand known? Amiya wondered.

"Her class is going to represent India," her mother explained to Daddy. "Miss Ferdinand thought you would be excited about that," she said to Amiya. "Don't you want to carry the Indian flag in the parade?"

"No," Amiya said.

"Why not?" Daddy asked.

Amiya shrugged. "I just don't." How could she explain? She had worked so hard to be *normal*. At school, she often forgot she had brown skin and black hair and that she ate strange food at home. How could she march in the parade and remind all the kids that she was *not normal*?

"You should be proud that the teacher has chosen India." Her mother smoothed back a lock of Amiya's hair.

Amiya didn't answer.

"Miss Ferdinand says that if you do not want to do India, she will choose another country."

Amiya glanced at her mother.

"What shall I tell her?" Mommy asked.

"Yes."

"Yes, what?"

"Yes. Choose another country."

Her mother sighed.

*

Miss Ferdinand was again standing at the front of the room with her hands clasped in front of her chest. She was not smiling this time. "We have a change of plans," she said. "Instead of India, I have decided to choose—" she extended her arm in another direction— "Italy. Jessie's great-grandparents came to this country from Italy. Jessie will carry the Italian flag in the parade."

All heads, including Amiya's, turned to stare at Jessie, who sat up tall and grinned at everyone. Jessie was so pretty, it didn't matter if her family was from another country. And Italy was not a strange country like India. They ate pizza in Italy.

*

"Quiet!" The principal clapped her hands. All the kids in the entire school were sitting on the floor in the cafeteria, with the gray metal tables pushed to the sides of the room. Each set of tables had one mother standing next to it. Amiya's mother stood next to the India tables: Vinod's class.

"Quiet!" The principal clapped again. "Your teacher will tap you on the shoulder when it is time for you to go to your tables. Then the parade will begin."

When Miss Ferdinand tapped her shoulder, Amiya pushed and shoved her way to their tables with the rest of her class. She wanted everyone to see that she was *not* going to the India tables.

Each class had three tables. One of theirs displayed mini pizza rolls that Jessie's mother made; on another was a large square of lace and some glass paperweights with little glass flowers floating in them; and the last table had some books from the library about Italy. The students had made the posters on the wall behind the tables: how to count in Italian; how to say hello and goodbye and thank you in Italian.

The parade arrived. Amiya didn't want to look for Vinod, but she did, and there he was: the only brown boy in the line, holding the orange and green Indian flag with the blue wheel in the center. Vinod was smiling. The parade marched around the room.

"Jessie! Jessie!" Amiya's class yelled. The second time around, Jessie stepped out of line and lowered her flagpole into the holder on the floor.

Amiya's eyes followed Vinod around the room, until his flag was in its holder. Amiya's mother had covered the India tables with yellow cloth. She had made milk-powder burfees and brought Indian money, an Indian leather purse, a beautiful little carved lamp, a map, and lots of other things.

"Hey, Amiya. I'll trade you."

Cheryl, at the next set of tables, held out a cube of cheese on a toothpick. Cheryl's country was Norway, and they had a bunch of candleholders and sweaters on one of their tables.

"I'll trade you for a pizza roll," Cheryl said.

"We're not supposed to," Amiya said.

"Why not?"

"We have to wait our turn to go around the room."

"Then save me a piece," she said.

Amiya glanced at the tray. Jessie's mother stood right next to it. "I can't," Amiya said.

"OK," Cheryl agreed cheerfully. She opened her mouth and popped in the cheese.

Across the cafeteria, Vinod's friends pressed their palms together and shouted "Namaste!" One of the girls in Vinod's class was dressed in a sari. It wasn't really a sari. It was a child's

costume, with the sari pleats already sewn in. You just tied it
on. The girl wore this over her T-shirt, and she had a round
red self-stick kumkum on her forehead. She looked ridiculous.
Amiya was so embarrassed for her. There was nothing Indian
about her at all.

Amiya wondered if there was really nothing Italian about
her class's table. And nothing Norwegian about Cheryl's table.
Maybe the international fair was just—American.

*

"Only one more week of school," Cheryl said.

Amiya and Cheryl were at the playground near the townhouses. They'd been taking turns jumping off the swings, and
now they sat on the grass.

Cheryl plucked a dandelion. "Do you like butter?" She
held the dandelion under Amiya's chin.

"What?"

"If you like butter, the dandelion will make your skin
yellow."

"Does it?"

Cheryl tipped her head and peered. "I can't tell."

"Let me try." Amiya took the dandelion and held it under
Cheryl's chin.

"Is it yellow?" Cheryl asked.

"I don't know. Maybe."

"Here." Cheryl rubbed the flower firmly over the skin
under Amiya's chin. "Now it's yellow."

"Isn't that cheating?"

"No." Cheryl plucked another dandelion and scrubbed it
under her own chin. "Look." She tipped her head back.

Amiya saw a light smear of yellow. "Yeah," she said.

Cheryl threw the dandelion away. She walked on her knees

closer to Amiya. "I wish I had hair like yours." She stroked Amiya's hair. "So long and shiny."

"Your hair would be just like mine if you let it grow," Amiya assured her.

"You think so?"

"Sure. Your hair is straight." Amiya lifted a few strands of Cheryl's light brown hair. "Mine is straight. Grow it out, and you'll look just like me."

"Really?" Cheryl grinned.

"Yeah. I promise."

REVOLUTION

Neel was thirteen and his sister, Anita, was ten, when their parents split up. On a chilly day in March, his mother picked him up after his astronomy club meeting and told him. As he sat in the front seat listening to her, Neel tried to keep his mind on the fact that he, his mother, the car, and the freeway were, at that moment, spinning through space at 30 kilometers per second on their journey around the sun.

In the months before the divorce was final, when Dad had moved out and was living on the other side of Newark in an unfurnished efficiency apartment, which contained almost nothing but a beanbag chair and empty Chinese food takeout boxes, Neel asked his parents many times why they were getting divorced.

His father, T. Gopalakrishnan, would rub his small pot belly slowly and say, in his thick Indian accent, rolling his R's and enunciating each consonant strongly, "Your mother has decided she does not want to be married to me anymore."

His mother, Linda, would toss her long brown hair over her shoulder and say, "Your father isn't interested in working on our marriage."

Neel tried to point out to each parent that, apparently, things could work out if they simply admitted to each other that they wanted to stay married. They'd shake their heads and look at him searchingly. "No, Neel," they'd say. "It won't work. I'm sorry."

He was baffled by the ways of adults. One day, while he and Anita were sitting on the floor of the basement rec room playing Monopoly, he asked, "How can two people get a divorce without ever having a fight?"

Anita moved her piece, the horse, past "Go" and counted $200 onto her pile of money. "They fought all the time."

"When?"

"They fought every day. Didn't you hear them?"

Neel thought about this. He remembered a chilliness in the air during dinners sometimes. He remembered his parents closing their bedroom door and having muffled conversations. He remembered wanting to retreat to his room more often than usual.

"What did they fight about?" he asked.

"Mom said Dad was spoiled and expected to be treated like a prince. She said she wasn't a subservient Indian wife. Dad said he only wanted a hot meal and a clean house when he came home, and that Mom was the spoiled one. He said she wanted to be waited on hand and foot. Mom said all she wanted was for Dad to pay attention. She said he didn't even know which days the trash was picked up. She said he never remembered her birthday or their anniversary. Mom said they needed marriage counseling and Dad said he'd never set foot in a counselor's office. He said there was nothing wrong with him. It's your turn, Neel."

"How did you hear all that?"

"My room is next to theirs. I could hear everything."

Neel was astonished that Anita could remember all this. He didn't see how these minor misunderstandings could lead to something as momentous as ripping apart the only life he'd ever known. He thought his parents were hiding something from him.

One day, he stormed home from school. "Is he having an affair?" he demanded. His voice cracked, both from emotion and from his enlarging voice box.

"Who?" Mom asked. She was sitting at the kitchen table, which had been, since Dad moved out, piled high with papers which Neel and Anita were not to touch, and which never went away. "These are important financial documents," his mother would say. "We need these for the divorce." The table in the dining room was, as usual, covered with potted plants. It was the sunniest room in the house. So, they'd been eating their dinners on the sofa in the family room.

"Dad," Neel said. He was standing with his jacket and shoes still on, when normally the rule at their house had been to take off shoes as soon as you walked in the door. That was an Indian habit, and his father liked to point out that taking off one's shoes was a way to make a distinction between the stress of work and school, and the comforts of home.

Now that Dad wasn't around, Neel noticed that even his mother was clomping around the entire house in her sneakers.

"Of course not," Mom said, looking back at the papers in front of her. "Where did you get that idea?"

"Jay Benmer at school said Dad must be having an affair. That's why his cousin's parents got a divorce and they wouldn't tell his cousin the truth for a long time."

Mom shook her head. "It's nothing like that. We are telling

you the truth."

"I don't get it."

"Sit down." She pushed aside a pile of papers, took hold of his hand across the table, and looked him in the eye. He knew they were now going to have a serious, adult conversation.

"When Gopi and I got married," she said in a measured tone, "we were so young. We were still in college. He was working on his PhD and I was a nursing student. We had no idea what we were getting into. Our backgrounds were so different. He's from Bangalore, which as you know is a huge city. I'm a small-town girl from Michigan."

Neel had heard this story many times. His parents had met when Dad started tutoring Mom in chemistry. "But you fell in love," he pointed out.

"At least we thought it was love. It may have been nothing more than loneliness."

"What d'you mean?"

"Maybe I shouldn't be telling you all this. College was such a big place for me. I hardly knew anyone. I missed my boyfriend from high school. We'd broken up when he decided to go into the Air Force, and I went off to nursing school. One day, during our tutoring session, I started crying. Gopi invited me up to the graduate student dorm and made dinner for me. I still remember it. He made a curry with nine kinds of vegetables. I was impressed that he knew how to cook a meal from scratch, and that he used so many vegetables. The boys I'd gone to high school with could barely make themselves a hot dog." She laughed. "Gopi was different from other boys I knew. He was so quiet and courteous. I thought he was really exotic." Mom rubbed Neel's fingers and smiled at her memories.

"Why are you getting a divorce?" Neel repeated.

Her smile faded. "Do you know why we got married so young?"

"Because you loved each other."

"Because I got pregnant."

Neel's hand flinched away from his mother's, but she had a tight warm grip on his fingers. His eyes rested on a document that said "Statement of Assets" across the top.

"Is this too much for you to know?" she asked.

He mumbled something and shrugged.

"I thought I might as well tell you, since you seem so upset about the whole thing. We knew our families wouldn't be happy about our marriage, so we just went to the Justice of the Peace and then told everyone about it later."

Neel's forehead began to furrow. "But I wasn't born until—" He wondered if, somehow, his parents had lied to him about his birth date to make things appear more normal.

"Oh!" she laughs. "It wasn't you. I ended up having a miscarriage. That's the ironic part. If we'd waited even another month, we probably never would have gotten married at all."

Neel wasn't entirely sure what a miscarriage was—whether it was an accidental event or a deliberate action. "Did you think about getting a divorce then?" he asked.

"No. We both come from families where no one ever gets divorced."

"Then why get one now?"

She let go of his hand. "I'm older now. I don't want to keep waiting and hoping things will get better."

"What things?"

"Your father—" she licked her lips. She shook her head. "No. I can't tell you all this. Your father's a good man. I want you to remember that, Neel. OK?" She patted his hand and gave him a tight smile. The serious, adult talk was over.

*

During the process of the divorce, Neel grew taller than his dad. By the time everything was final, he was thin and lanky, bent like a willow tree in the wind.

The summer before his ninth-grade year, he and Anita moved with their mother to Centerton, Michigan, a small town about two hours southwest of Ann Arbor. Centerton was where his mother had grown up and where Neel's Grandma Mary and Grandpa Paul still lived.

"This is the first divorce our family has ever known," Grandma Mary said. Neel, his sister, and his mother were sitting around her blue-speckled Formica kitchen table the night they arrived. They were staying there until they found a place to live. The kitchen was small and old and smelled of roast beef and bacon. They sat in the darkness, except for the light from the stove. Moonlight streamed through the lace curtains, making a pattern of lacy light and shadows on the table. Anita traced the bright circles with her finger. Grandma placed a long white cigarette between her lips and flicked her lighter, which flared brilliantly in the dimness.

"I didn't think anything good would come of marrying a foreigner." Grandma tapped her cigarette into an empty coffee mug. She had sold all her ashtrays at a garage sale some years ago, intending to quit smoking, so now she had to use whatever was handy for an ashtray.

"Mom," Linda said sternly.

"They're old enough to hear this."

"He's their *father*," Linda said. "*They're* the good that came out of the marriage."

Neel stood up abruptly and pushed open the back screen door. It slammed closed behind him. He stepped away from the house, away from the troublesome conversation inside. The air was warm, and the moon above, so bright and large, seemed close enough to touch. He remembered looking through the telescope during astronomy club one night and seeing with startling clearness the ring-shaped craters on the gray surface of the moon. Those craters were up there now, although he couldn't see them.

*

In Centerton, Neel and Anita were just about the only dusky-skinned people around. Not that anyone was prejudiced or anything. Adults went out of their way to be friendly to them. A few weeks after they arrived, at the beginning of ninth grade, Neel's homeroom teacher, Ms. Pierce, put her hand on his arm as he was getting ready to go to his first-period biology class. "Neel, what is your background?" she asked.

Neel shook his hair out of his eyes and said, "Pardon?"

"Your ethnic background," said Ms. Pierce. She was a young, slim woman with her hair in a ponytail, and a wide smile.

"Oh. Um, I'm half-Indian."

"How interesting!" She clasped her hands and bounced on her toes. "I'm part native myself. What tribe?"

He shook his head. "No. I mean, my dad's from India."

"I'm sorry, I misunderstood. That's fascinating. You might want to talk with Mr. Cartig. He'd like more diversity on the staff of the school newspaper. I'm sure you'd bring an unusual perspective."

Neel thought it might be fun to be on the school newspaper staff. There was no astronomy club at this school. But he didn't know how he could bring an "unusual perspective" to the paper. In New Jersey, there were so many kids with two Indian parents that he and Anita were viewed as hardly Indian at all.

*

In the spring of Neel's ninth-grade year, soon after his fifteenth birthday, Dad announced that he was going to take Neel and Anita to India over the summer. "We have not gone since you were eleven, Neel, and Anita was only eight," Dad pointed out.

Anita, on the extension upstairs in Mom's bedroom, wailed, "You said I could go to horse camp this summer!"

"Yes, yes," Dad said. "We will go to India at a different time from your horse camp."

"I don't want to go to India!" Anita wailed.

"Don't be such a baby," Neel said.

"You will have fun in India," Dad said.

"No, I won't." Anita sniffled.

"Yes, you will. Tell her, Neel. She will have fun, right?"

"Sure," Neel said. He didn't really want to go to India either, but he also didn't want to cause trouble.

Neel's mom was much more excited about the trip. "What a wonderful opportunity for the two of you!" she gushed when she heard about the plans.

"I'm not going," Anita said.

Mom bought several books about India for Neel and Anita: about Mahatma Gandhi and the Indian independence movement, about Indian holidays and festivals, about Indian geography. Mom even rented the movie *Gandhi*. Neel liked the character of Gandhi. He seemed kind and wise at the same time. Anita refused to look at any of the books, and wouldn't even watch the movie.

Neel told Mr. Cartig, the school newspaper advisor, that he was going to India over the summer. Neel was a "junior writer" on the school newspaper. Mr. Cartig's eyes lit up. "The land of Gandhi!" he declared. "You're a lucky kid, Neel, to have a personal connection with that man. He's perhaps the greatest leader since Jesus."

A personal connection to Gandhi. The greatest leader since Jesus. All day after he talked with Mr. Cartig, Neel wondered if this could be true. He had never been particularly proud of his Indian heritage. He hadn't been ashamed of it either. He just hadn't thought much about it. Now Mr. Cartig suggested there might be more to his family than he realized. That night, he told Dad what Mr. Cartig said.

Dad laughed. "Maybe Gandhi was the greatest leader since Jesus. But unfortunately, our family has no personal connection with him. Gandhi's family was from Gujarat. That's a completely different part of the country than where I grew up."

Neel felt hot with embarrassment at his father's laughter. "I'm sure Mr. Cartig didn't mean a personal connection as in, *related* or anything," he emphasized dramatically. "He just meant, you know, the same country and all."

"Same country," his father repeated. "Yes. OK, so are you ready for our trip?"

The next day, Neel told Mr. Cartig that his family had no personal connection with Gandhi. "He's from a completely different part of the country than my family," Neel informed Mr. Cartig, proud that he knew something about his own heritage.

Mr. Cartig said, "But your family must have been involved with the Indian independence movement. That was going on all over the country."

Neel nodded. He had never thought of that. When Dad called that evening Neel asked casually, "Were you involved in the Indian independence movement?"

Dad laughed harder and longer than before. Finally, he said, "I wasn't even born when India got independence!"

Neel cursed his own stupidity. How could he not have

known? After he got off the phone, he looked in his book again and found out that India won independence in 1947. Dad was born in 1958. So, it was Neel's *grandfather* who must have been part of the independence movement.

At Mr. Cartig's suggestion, Neel decided to interview his grandfather on this trip. It would be a real coup for a sophomore to have a feature article printed in the school newspaper. He packed a voice recorder and notebook in his suitcase.

In the end, Anita refused to come along, and Mom reluctantly agreed that she could spend time with Dad in New Jersey before the trip, but would come back to Michigan when Neel and Dad left for India.

*

"How are you, young man? I remember when you were only so high."

"He has grown tall! Do you remember us from your last trip to India?"

Neel's head was still spinning from the long plane ride and then the hair-raising taxi ride from the Bangalore airport. He and his dad stood in the entrance hallway of Dad's childhood home at three o'clock in the morning. Neel shifted his weight from one foot to the other and hung his head. Sriram Uncle clapped him on the back and Sunita Auntie pinched his cheek. He tossed his hair out of his face and tried to mumble something polite to his relatives.

Ahead of them on the wall was the garlanded black-and-white portrait of his grandmother, who died when Neel was a small boy. He didn't remember her. To the right of the photo was the shiny wooden door leading to his grandfather's room. Neel felt like a journalist on a foreign assignment, scoping out the scene. He'd put up with the discomforts of his assignment for the reward of seeing his words in print.

Over the next week, Neel tried to figure out how to arrange
an interview with his grandfather. Thatha was a large, bulky
man with a gigantic square head hanging from his frame. He
reminded Neel of a bison. He wore a white dhoti wrapped
around his legs (it looked like a long skirt to Neel), an under-
shirt, and a thin white towel neatly folded and draped over one
shoulder.

Several times a day Thatha walked majestically around the
house, hands behind his back, as though leading a procession.
Every so often, as he passed Neel perched on a sofa reading
old *Reader's Digest* magazines (the only reading material he
found in the house), Thatha barked out a question. "What is
the square root of 1,369?" "What is the name of the largest
volcano in the world?" After each question he glared at Neel
for a few seconds. As Neel floundered for an answer, Thatha
made a rumbling sound in his throat. Neel was never sure if
this was a chuckle or a cough. Then Thatha put out a massive
thick-veined hand and dropped a piece of foil-wrapped candy
into Neel's lap. Neel remembered that Thatha liked to produce
chocolate or caramel chewy candies at random moments and
watch his grandchildren squeal with delight. Neel was too old
for that kind of behavior now.

How was Neel supposed to interview a man like that?
Besides his frightening looks and manner, there was his in-
violable schedule, for which Sunita Auntie made elaborate
accommodations. Thatha must have hot coffee the minute he
woke up, so Auntie was constantly on the alert for that event.
After coffee, Thatha took his bath, and Auntie mixed his bath
water in the bucket to the exact temperature, placed a stool in
a particular spot on the granite bathroom floor, and made sure
Thatha's soap and shaving equipment were within easy reach.
After bathing, Thatha sat in the pooja room reciting prayers

and going through his ritual worship, for which Auntie provided fresh jasmine garlands, fruits, and cotton wicks dipped in ghee. After pooja, a full meal (rice, rasam, sambar, cooked vegetables, pickle, yogurt). Then, a walk to the post office or a store to do a few errands. Then a thorough reading of two or three newspapers. Then a nap, and afterwards, tea and snacks. It went on like this all day.

One afternoon, Neel asked his father about interviewing Thatha. Dad shook his head and said, "Not now. Later." Even though it was afternoon, Dad had just bathed and shaved and was getting dressed in a white embroidered Indian shirt. Neel wasn't sure what was up. Dad had done this once before—gotten dressed up and then disappeared for a few hours.

After Dad left, Neel found Sunita Auntie in the kitchen. She was making tea. It took a few tries before she understood what he wanted. His American accent was difficult for her, and she continued pouring and mixing as he talked. But when he mentioned the words "publish an article," she stopped her work and looked at him. "You want to interview your Thatha for an article in your school newspaper?" she asked. "Yes, we must arrange for that." She immediately walked into the living room, where Thatha was opening the mail and waiting for his tea.

That very day, after tea, Thatha and Neel retired to Thatha's bedroom. Thatha sat in a rattan chair with his hands gripping its arms, as though bracing himself for the work ahead. Neel sat on the bed and placed his voice recorder on the desk next to Thatha. He pushed the "record" button, opened his notebook, cleared his throat, and said, "I want to know what you did for India's independence."

"What?" Thatha shouted.

Neel repeated his question louder.

"What *I* did? I did nothing." Thatha sat back and looked

satisfied at having dispatched the first question so quickly.

Neel didn't know what to say to this. Thatha must have misunderstood the question. To buy a few minutes, Neel peered at the voice recorder. The red numbers kept counting the seconds relentlessly, recording nothing but the silence in the air.

Neel cleared his throat again and asked, slowly and loudly, "I mean, how did you help when India was trying to get independence?"

"I did not help," Thatha boomed again. "Our state was not under British rule. We had a Maharaja. Don't you know anything? What do they teach you in school over there in America?"

Neel's face flushed. He couldn't think of anything else to ask. His whole interview was demolished almost before it had begun. Why did none of his books mention this fact about the Maharaja?

"What else?" Thatha shouted. "Speak up."

"So . . ." Neel thought quickly, "the Maharaja was independent of the British government?" The question came out with a squeak at the end.

"No, of course not. Nothing was independent of the British. The Maharajas ruled only with British consent."

"Then why didn't anyone in this state do anything for independence?"

"Oh, many people did things. There were all sorts of marches and speeches. That sort of thing."

Neel was confused by his grandfather's responses. Thatha shifted his weight impatiently and his chair creaked. Neel hurried to think of a question. "Did you like the British?" he asked.

"The British modernized India," Thatha proclaimed. "Our railways were built by the British. Do you know India's railway system employs more people than any other institution in the world?"

"So . . . do you think the British should have stayed in India?" Neel didn't want to think his grandfather was a British sympathizer, but after all, if it was true, it might result in an interesting article anyway.

Thatha rumbled loudly and slammed a fist onto the desk, causing the voice recorder to fall onto the hard ground. "Of course not. What kind of question is that? Nobody wants to be colonized. You must know America was a British colony at one time. You people didn't like it any better. Don't you know about the American revolution?"

Neel picked up the recorder. The numbers continued to tick off the seconds. He set it on the table again.

"The British looted this country!" Thatha continued. "You know they took our cotton to England, had it made into cloth there, and then brought it here and forced us to buy it!"

Neel knew. He read it in one of his books. He felt a glimmer of hope. Maybe the interview wasn't dead yet. "Did you burn British-made cloth?" He had read about the huge bonfires Indians made out of British clothes and toys.

Thatha shook his massive head. "No, no. I did no such thing."

"Why not?" Neel's frustration was rising. "Didn't you want freedom for India?"

"Of course. Why do you go on asking the same question over and over again?"

"Because I don't understand. Why didn't you help out? Was it dangerous to help?"

"It was not so dangerous. You must remember, the British were not Nazis. They jailed people who were public about their support of independence. If you attended rallies and made a fuss, they might jail you. In your own home, you could burn as many British clothes as you wanted. They would not bother you."

"So why didn't you?"

Thatha slammed his fist again. The recorder fell again, and Neel let it stay on the floor. "I told you already," Thatha boomed. "Our state was under the Maharaja. There was no need for me to do anything. Gandhi had so many people helping him. What good would it have done for me to burn a few clothes? Hmm?"

Thatha's logic seemed water-tight. Neel could think of nothing else to ask. But he wanted an article. He tried one last time. "What have you done that you are most proud of?"

"Hm? Proud? No, I am not a proud man. 'Pride goeth before the fall.' Who said that?" He glared at Neel for an instant, and then continued. "I am a modest man. I mind my own business. I don't get involved in anything and everything that is going on around me. That is how I have always lived my life."

Thatha stood up, turned his back on Neel, and proceeded to re-tuck his dhoti. Then he stalked out of the room. The interview was obviously over.

Neel rescued the recorder from the floor, turned it off, gathered his things and climbed up the stairs to the bedroom he and his father shared. He hurled his recorder and notebook on the bed. They didn't even bounce, the mattress was so thin. Then he hauled his suitcase out from under the bed, scooped up the recorder and notebook, threw them in there, and shoved the suitcase back under the bed. He sat down on the bed. He stood up again. Shaking his head, he dragged the suitcase out again. Squatting on the floor, he turned on the recorder, pressed the "erase" button and held it until the number flipped to zero. He threw it all back into his suitcase, zipped it closed, and pushed it far under the bed once more. He flung himself face-down on the hard bed.

*

Just before dinner, Dad turned on the light in the bed-room. Neel woke up and squinted at him. Dad was smiling broadly.

Neel rubbed his eyes. "What's going on, Dad?"

"It's all settled! I will be married soon."

"What?" Neel sat up cross-legged on the bed.

"I have been corresponding with one woman for some months. Her name is Madhupushpa. We had our horoscopes matched by an astrologer, and now I have met her twice." Dad was walking around the room, waving his arms. "She is a widow with one daughter. You will meet her tomorrow. We are invited there for lunch and you must be on your best behavior. You must try to eat everything she serves you. Understand?" Dad didn't wait for an answer, but continued talking breath-lessly. "We will be married in a few days at the temple near her house. Just a simple wedding, since it is a second marriage for both of us. I have decided to do things the Indian way this time. When you have Indian blood, you must do things the Indian way."

His father caught sight of himself in a mirror on the steel clothing cabinet. He stopped in front of his image, smoothed his hand over his mostly bald head, and smiled at himself.

Neel leaped off the bed and lunged at his father, grabbing handfuls of the white embroidered shirt. He towered over his father. "Why didn't you tell me?" he screamed. "Why didn't you tell me before we got here?"

His father took several steps to regain his balance and grasped Neel's wrists. "Neel, stop it," Dad said, pushing him down on the bed. "I am surprised at you. You have always been a good boy. Now you are behaving like Anita. I did not know myself I was going to get married until this afternoon. How could I have told you any sooner?" Neel lunged up again, and Dad pushed him back down again.

"Why didn't you tell me you were writing letters?" Neel screamed from his position on the bed. Dad's hands pressed onto his shoulders, keeping him down. Dad was short but strong. "This whole trip was so you could get married, wasn't it?"

"I did not want to upset you, Neel," Dad said in a calm, even voice. "The divorce has been hard on you. I know that. I did not want to tell you something that might not happen. I thought it would be best if I waited until everything was final. You are still a child. You do not need to be burdened with knowing about your father's marriage plans."

"You burdened me with the divorce!" Neel screamed.

Dad took his hands away and stepped back. "Yes," he sighed. "We did. We could not help it. I'm sorry, Neel."

Dad slowly began removing his shirt and pants. He folded his clothes and wrapped a dhoti around his legs. He slipped on an old plaid shirt. As he dressed, Dad said, "My marriage will make no difference in your life. I will still call you every evening. You will still come to visit me during your school vacations. Now, Madhupushpa Auntie will be able to make a more comfortable home for you, with home-cooked food and all. You will like it."

Neel slumped on the bed. Dad's marriage would make no difference in his life. That was the problem. He wanted there to be a difference—a good difference—in his life.

"I think you will like Madhupushpa." Dad patted Neel on the back. "Come down with me and have dinner."

Neel shook his head. "I'm not hungry." He lay back on the bed. Dad walked out of the room, leaving the door open and the light on.

Outside, a peacock screamed and auto rickshaws sputtered.

Neel stared up at the ceiling, trying to create pictures out of the random cracks spider-webbing across the white paint. Maybe he was too good. He should throw a tantrum now, refuse to meet this lady, Madhu-whatever, insist that Dad take him back home immediately. That's what Anita would do.

Neel became aware of heavy footsteps in the hall. Dad must be coming back. Neel closed his eyes. He didn't want to interact with Dad.

Something rumbled. Neel opened his eyes to see Thatha standing in the door. He'd never known Thatha to come upstairs before.

"You are not hungry?" Thatha demanded.

Neel sat up. He didn't want Thatha to think he was disrespectful. "Not really," he said.

"Our food does not agree with you." Thatha sat down on the bed beside Neel. He rubbed his hands on the towel slung over his shoulder and grumbled softly in his throat. Neel wasn't sure what to say or do.

"Your father is getting remarried," Thatha observed.

"Yeah."

"I do not understand the ways of the modern world. Divorce is very difficult for the youngsters." Thatha said the word "die-vorce."

"I don't understand it either," Neel said.

Thatha put out a massive fist. Neel wasn't sure what to do. Was Thatha trying to give him a fist bump? Then Neel realized—he was about to drop a piece of candy.

But before Neel could open his palm to accept the gift, Thatha withdrew his fist to his lap and rubbed it with his other hand. "You are growing up," he growled.

Neel nodded stupidly.

"You are very studious," Thatha declared. "You will go far in life."

"Thank you," Neel said, his voice crackling.

Thatha kept massaging his fist and rumbling, as though he wished to say more. Then, he abruptly stood up and lumbered out of the room. At the doorway he said, without turning around, "You come down and ask Sunita Auntie to make you something else for dinner. She will not mind. It is not good to go to bed hungry."

"Thank you," Neel said again.

As Thatha's footsteps thudding downstairs, Neel felt a lump in his throat, and his eyes stung. He swiped at them furiously.

A small gray lizard scampered lightning-quick across the wall opposite. Then it backed up and turned, as though looking at him. Neel clapped, and the creature shot into a crack behind the bookcase. At least he had the power to scare a small animal.

The lizard poked its head out. Neel lay down on the bed, hands behind his head, feet still on the floor, watching the tiny reptile zipper along the wall. He thought about clapping again, but decided to let the lizard be.

He, and the lizard, and his father, and his grandfather were all co-passengers on this planet, speeding along at 30 kilometers per second around the sun. His mother, his sister, his teachers—even Madhupushpa—everyone was on this reeling circuit with him. And the entire solar system was revolving around the center of the galaxy, which was in turn moving through space.

Neel closed his eyes and imagined himself into a very, very tiny speck in black space. He contracted himself into a smaller and smaller dot, until he almost didn't even exist. Then he thrust this dot into orbit, faster and faster. He was a miniscule amount of matter, flying through space at an unimaginable velocity. He knew this was actually true—yet he couldn't feel a thing.

DREAMS

Don't say it, Malini thinks as she spoons up her cereal and milk. Across the table, her twin brother stabs his cornflakes with the tip of his spoon. "I dreamed," he begins. His voice is a loud drone. "I was driving a race car in the desert, and going incredibly fast, way way too fast, and everything was passing me in a total black blur."

He wears an old pair of sweatpants and no shirt. He's so thin, he looks like a question mark above his cereal bowl. Malini does not want to hear about another of his terrifying dreams.

"And no matter how hard I stomped on the brakes," he chants, "the car wouldn't slow down, and the steering wheel didn't work either, and then I was heading for the edge of this cliff and I still couldn't stop, and—"

"I hope that is not how you will be driving next year," their father booms. "If so, maybe we will have to put off the driver's education."

No one laughs. Pramod hangs his head over his cereal bowl.

Dad puts a little finger into his ear and wiggles it furiously.

Mom lifts her spoon to her mouth, chews, and swallows. "Did you sleep well last night?" she murmurs to Pramod.

Pramod stuffs an enormous spoonful of cereal in his mouth. He shakes his head.

"He has not been sleeping properly." Mom looks at Dad for his reaction.

Dad sweeps his eyes over the table. "What you kids need is more exercise," he proclaims. "That is why you cannot sleep well."

Malini opens her mouth to say something. It annoys her when Mom and Dad group her and Pramod together. *She's* not having trouble sleeping. Just because they're twins, doesn't mean they're the same person. But she doesn't say anything.

"Too much sitting around," Dad continues. "Couch potato, that is what they call it in this country. Are we going to become a bunch of couch potato bondas?"

Still, no one laughs except Dad, who forces out a chuckle. They've heard this joke intermittently for weeks, whenever Pramod admits he hasn't slept well. Malini dips her spoon into her cereal bowl and sips the sweet milk. She's not hungry, but doesn't want to call attention to herself by leaving the table first. Her eyes roam over the wallpaper with tomatoes and peppers, and, beside the fridge, the built-in cutting board which Mom has converted into a pooja area. There are tiny silver deepas and a matching incense stick holder in front of a prominent picture of Lord Venkateshvara.

Dad leaves the table first. His bowl and coffee cup remain on the table. He's already dressed for work. He stands in front of the pooja area with palms together for a few moments. He squats down to kneel and bob his forehead to the floor three times, as usual, and then dots his forehead with red kumkum powder. From the front hallway, he calls out "I'll be back" in Kannada to Mom.

Pramod leaves the table next. He also doesn't put his bowl in the sink. He scrapes his chair back and pounds up the stairs. The bathroom door slams shut and the shower bursts on.

The kitchen is so quiet that Malini can hear her mother chewing. When Mom has tipped her bowl to scoop up the last spoonful of milk, she rises and stacks Pramod's and Dad's bowls into her own. The dishes clink as she rinses and arranges them in the dishwasher. "You'll be late," she reminds Malini as she returns for the coffee cups. "Go, I'll do it for you."

Malini leaves her almost-full bowl for her mother to empty and rinse, and climbs the stairs to the bathroom, still steaming from Pramod's shower. She's already dressed in a pair of jeans and a sweatshirt with faded letters reading, "Rock & Roll Hall of Fame." She brushes her teeth and then looks at herself in the mirror, trying to picture in her mind how others at school will see her. One other in particular: Rob Griffin. There's a small white pimple on her chin. She leans closer to the mirror and dabs antiseptic-smelling cream on the zit. She rolls a tube of lip gloss over her lips. She grabs her books and purse from her bedroom and heads out the door.

She's standing at the bus stop clutching her books to her chest when Pramod runs up behind her. He's carrying nothing. She turns her head to him, but the rest of her body still faces front, where the bus will pull up any minute. "How come you never have any books?"

Pramod shrugs.

"What's with all the weird dreams you've been having?"

"I d'know."

"Why do you tell us about them every morning?"

He doesn't answer, but turns to Jared behind him and

punches the boy on the arm. Jared is a flabby, talkative boy who lives on the next block.

"Hey, Pramod," Jared says, punching back. "You gonna fail another math quiz today, or did you study?"

Malini faces front. She doesn't want to know that her brother is failing math quizzes. Sometimes she hears these things about her brother. The high school is so big that they don't have any classes together, but still some of her friends know some kids in his classes, and once, a few months ago, Jared came up to her in the hallway and said, "Your brother's crazy, you know that?" Jared was laughing. "He's out in the maintenance shed smoking a cigarette."

At that time Malini didn't believe Jared, but ever since then, whenever she's in the vicinity of her brother, she sniffs quietly and sometimes she thinks she can smell cigarette smoke. Most times, though, he smells of peppermint candy.

*

Dr. Shastry has a busy day, as usual. He goes up to the pediatric oncology ward to do his rounds first. He looks at the chart of a teenaged girl bald from chemotherapy and reassures her parents that the treatment is proceeding appropriately. Next he visits the bed of a two-year-old boy who's had surgery and has his hands restrained so he won't pull at his dressing or his IV. The mother sobs in the corner. Dr. Shastry checks the boy's incision and medication level and, in the hallway, tells the nurse, "Get that mother out of there. Doesn't he have any other relative who can be with him?" He also sees John Craig, a fifteen-year-old boy who is dying. The parents, one on each side of the bed, stand up as he comes in. Their faces are calm and attentive. He has known these parents for years, has always admired their strength, and now the time has come to talk to them about hospice care for their son. "I'm sorry," he says to Mr. and Mrs. Craig. His voice cracks. They bow their heads.

His appointments for the day include a child who's been referred with a possible brain tumor; and a follow-up visit with an eleven-year-old leukemia patient who's doing well, considering, but whose parents are divorcing due to the stress of caring for her.

In the afternoon Dr. Shastry goes to Summit County Children's Services for his once-a-week volunteer shift. He sees kids in foster care who have colds and acne and athlete's foot, and one four-year-old boy with a bruised back. The mother's boyfriend is being investigated for child abuse.

*

Mrs. Shastry has a usual day. It's Tuesday, wash day, so after she cleans the kitchen from breakfast, she goes down to the basement and sorts the clothes into four piles. She has noticed, for some time, a faint smell of cigarettes coming from the kids' clothes, and she wonders about these American schools, where they must allow the teachers to smoke. What kind of example is that for the children?

After she loads the washer, she sits in the living room and works on one of her knitted caps for the preemie babies at her husband's hospital. Several years ago, she volunteered for a few weeks in the preemie ward, holding the tiny babies, like tiny hairless puppies. But she was so saddened by those babies that she cried every day when she came home. So, she signed up to make the caps and she's made dozens every year. Dr. Shastry sometimes comes home with a photo of a smiling child and says, "Here, this is one of the babies you held, and now he is doing just fine." Mrs. Shastry likes to see these photos, and she likes to think her caps are helping the babies grow up into smiling children, but she has never again gone into the preemie ward to see those hairless puppies.

After lunch (tomato soup and grilled cheese, as usual), she sits down in the family room to watch her soap opera, *The Lives We Live*, and to fold clothes. Skeletal Donna is plotting to kill innocent young Jennie because Jennie is engaged to marry Donna's ex-husband, Frank, whom Donna is still secretly in love with. Jennie is so innocent, she doesn't realize that Frank is two-timing her with her own sister, the racy Rachelle, who is a cocaine user and is about to be busted because she unknowingly sold some cocaine to an undercover police officer.

Mrs. Shastry enjoys spending an hour every day with these people. This is what America is really like! she thinks. After watching, she always feels glad to be Indian and not to have to worry about all those things.

*

Malini has a pretty good day, until the last period. Her first class is English. Today Rob Griffin sits in front of her and, when it's time to exchange papers to critique each other's work, he turns to her and smiles. As he gives her his paper, his cool, dry fingers brush her hand. All day long—as she takes neat, orderly notes; answers questions correctly; eats lunch with her best friends Amanda and Juliana; and learns about three-point perspective in art class—she remembers that smile and feels a warm thrill.

The last period of the day is a study hall for her. She sits in the vast lunchroom, wrapping her arms around herself against the chill, and with angles and sines and cosines swimming before her eyes, she remembers the feel of Rob's fingers on her hand.

"Hey, Malini." Someone jostles her shoulder. Jared sits

down beside her. "Your brother just got a three-day suspension." Jared is smirking.

"No, he didn't." She leans away from him.

"He did. For smoking on school property." Jared looks scornful and impressed at the same time.

The floor drops out of Malini's heart. It can't be true. Could it be true?

The bell rings, and Jared trots away. Malini watches herself rise calmly, gather her books to her chest, and leave the study hall. She gets on the school bus. Pramod is already slouched on the very back seat by the window, where he usually sits. She slides in beside him.

"Is it true what Jared said?" she whispers.

Pramod hands her two sheets of paper, the only things he's carrying. The first is a badly photocopied form, the letters thick and wiggly. Pramod's name has been filled in, as well as the date and the signature of Mrs. Grooley, the school counselor. Malini has never seen a suspension notice before.

The other piece of paper says "Summit County Family Resources" across the top. It lists things like the Food Stamp office and the Domestic Violence Prevention Center. One address is circled in thick, red marker: the Family Counseling Services office.

Malini stares at the heavy red circle for a long time. Then she whispers, "Does she think you need to get some counseling?"

Pramod leans his head against the side of the bus and closes his eyes. Malini can't tell if he's sleeping, or if he just doesn't want to talk to her.

She feels her throat tighten. She wipes her sleeve over her eyes, hoping no one will notice. Amanda gets on the bus, sees Malini sitting at the back with Pramod, and turns away. Rob Griffin gets on the bus. If he notices Malini way at the back, he gives no indication. Jared gets on the bus. He usually sits at the back with Pramod. Today, he doesn't even glance at them, but hurries into a seat near the front.

She's never even been friends with anyone who got a suspension, and now her own brother has one. Malini sits beside him, silent and upright, all the way home.

*

"No." Dad shakes his head.

They're at the dinner table. The kitchen smells of incense from the evening pooja, and warm rice, and fried mustard seeds. The white paper with the red circle is on the table in front of Dad, where Malini put it a moment ago. Pramod is upstairs sleeping.

"He does not need to see any counselor," Dad booms. "Pramod has been disobedient. He is being punished. He will learn. That is enough. These Americans are always running to counselors, and still they have problems. They cannot stay married to each other, not even when they have a sick child to take care of. Indians are different. We handle our own problems within the family. And in our family, we do not have such serious problems that we need to tell strangers about them."

"But he is failing his class." Mom is on the verge of tears. Her hands are in her lap and she hasn't touched the rice on her plate.

Malini puts out her hand and slides the white paper towards her.

"He will have to study harder, that is all," Dad declaims. "There is nothing wrong with him. He is a strong, healthy boy. He is just lazy. You know, I have a patient who is a boy of your age." He glares at Malini, as though she's also lazy and failing math class. "This fifteen-year-old boy is dying." Dad clears his throat. "There is nothing I can do for him." His voice softens. "We do not have such problems, thank God."

"Yes, thank God," Mom whispers.

Malini folds the white paper in her lap into half, and half again. She keeps folding until the red circle is no longer visible on the neat, thick packet of whiteness.

*

His wife shakes him. "He's still awake."

Dr. Shastry, eyes unfocused from sleep, squints at the illuminated digital clock on the nightstand: ten past two.

"Why don't you give him something?" she pleads in Kannada.

He rises onto his elbows. The bedroom is dark, but through the open door he can see, down the hall, a slice of light under Pramod's door.

"Some sleeping pill or something," she said. "Without sleep, how is he going to study well?"

"I don't believe in giving sleeping pills to children," Dr. Shastry grumbles. "He'll be OK."

His wife rolls over, tugging and arranging the covers. Dr. Shastry remains motionless. He watches that unwavering bar of light from under Pramod's door. He glances at the clock, waiting for the red number to change. Finally, at twenty past two, he hears his wife's soft snoring. Then he eases himself out from under the covers and walks slowly to Pramod's door. He lifts his hand to knock. He can hear, inside, papers rustling and a radio playing, very softly, music with an insistent drumbeat.

He puts his hand down. What good will it do for him to knock? Pramod will realize, eventually, that he must go to bed at a decent hour.

Dr. Shastry walks back into his own room and gets into

bed. The curtains are open and the crescent moon just visible at the bottom. Pramod is fine. He's just going through some sort of phase.

Dr. Shastry can't sleep, but he doesn't want to get out of bed until the usual time. He watches the moon as it inches up through the branches of the oak tree. Intermittently, he glances at the hallway, where light is still bleeding from under Pramod's door.

When the moon rises out of his view, he sees Pramod's light click off.

The darkness settles over Dr. Shastry like a blanket. He sighs, rolls over, and falls into a sleep full of dreams, none of which he will remember when he wakes up.

THE SWEATER

I don't care what Mom says—this is good yarn. It's directly from the sheep. No dyes, no treatments. Completely natural. Mom could care less about all of that, of course. I bought it from a woman who raises sheep near here. There was a craft fair on campus a few weeks ago, and she had a table there.

Mom asked, "Why did you buy such a dull color?" It's sort of a mottled tan, a mix of the white and black sheep wools. And she said, "It's so rough." Well, it's not lambswool.

I went to visit Mom and Dad last weekend. I don't know why I bothered. I guess I had nothing better to do, since Josh left. I didn't tell them about Josh leaving, of course. I'm not supposed to be dating him. I'm supposed to "get to know some nice Indian boys." I can't stand going to those India Student Association events, with everyone all concerned about who's going to make the most money.

Josh had to go home to help his mother sell her house and

move to an apartment. He's a pushover. His sister was supposed to help, and she backed out at the last minute. So, Josh
has to do it. He's been texting me almost every day. I haven't
replied yet, except to say, "Hey, everything's fine."

I'm sitting here in my room on the second floor, in an old
armchair someone left, and winding the yarn into a ball. This
yarn is sold in hanks, so you have to wind the balls yourself.
The trick is to always wrap the yarn around your hand. Then
when you take your hand out, there's some slack there, and you
haven't stretched the yarn too tight. The wool woman taught
me that. She knows all about yarn.

I hate this house I moved into. It was cheap, and I thought
it would be OK, but the other people are weird. There's one
guy who lives in the attic who covered the walls of his entire
room in black plastic. That's the kind of people I live with.

I was supposed to live with Josh this summer. That was the
plan. At least, it was *his* plan. I'd stay in town for the summer
and we'd live together, and our folks would never know. Instead, he got called away by his mother, so I'm alone.

It's kind of good to be alone. None of my friends are
around this summer—they've all gone home or gone off to do
some internship or job. It's OK. The town is quiet, of course.
They're doing a bunch of road repair and everything smells
like tar, and the sun blazes down and it's so humid, my T-shirt
sticks to my skin. Everything is wilted: the grass, the bushes, the
morning newspaper on the porch which someone subscribes
to. Even the parked cars seem to be slowly melting in the heat.

Things are so quiet, I can go all day without saying one
word to anyone—not even at work. I work the evening shift at
this place that transcribes news stories. It's kind of interesting,
I guess. Kind of boring, too. Mom and Dad think it's beneath
me. "You are just a secretary," Mom said. Well, duh. I haven't
even graduated college yet. What kind of job did they think I

was going to get?

So yesterday, I tried going the whole day without saying anything. I did my work silently and nodded to people who said hi to me. No one noticed.

When I'm not at work, I stay in my room. And the knitting is turning out to be good. I need a project to take my mind off things. Something to do during the day, until I have to go to work. I still can't believe the wool woman *made* this yarn. She's really into shearing the sheep and carding the wool and spinning it and all that stuff. She even has a collection of old spinning things, wheels and spindles. I don't know if I could ever get into anything as much as she's into wool.

So anyway, that's all Mom had to say to me about this yarn—something negative. Mom can't say anything to me that's not negative. I did what they wanted me to do. I'm a business major. Mom and Dad want me to apply to get an MBA and I took the GMAT, but my scores weren't high. So, I'm supposed to be studying this summer and taking the GMAT again this fall.

I don't know if I want to study business anymore. It would be crazy to quit now. I only have one more year, and my parents have paid a lot of money for my education. But I can't stand some of these up-and-coming jerks who are in school with me. They've already started buying their dress-for-success clothes for internship interviews. It makes me sick to see these people—who I've seen wasted drunk on the weekends—pretending to be so mature and all that, in their skirt suits and pantyhose and pumps.

I keep thinking, do clothes make you a better person? Does selling more orange juice or aspirin make you a better person? Of course not. On the other hand, I do buy things. I engage in trade. I enjoy shopping. And someone like the wool woman—she's in business for herself, isn't she? So business isn't all bad.

Maybe I should stick with it. I don't know.

It's crazy to knit a wool sweater in the summer. I found this knitting book at the used bookstore—*Knitting Without Tears*. The author gives you basic directions, but you design your own sweaters, based on your own knitting gauge and the size you want. Nothing like what Mom taught me, where I had to follow the directions exactly, knit each piece separately—the front, back and sleeves—and then sew everything together. The idea was that if you didn't follow the directions exactly, the sweater wouldn't come out right. But this book says, you can figure it out for yourself as you go along.

I'll start the sweater at the bottom and knit around to the armholes. I'll start the sleeves at the cuff and knit up to the underarm. Then I'll put all the stitches—from the body and both sleeves—on one large circular needle and start working the yoke. Afterwards, all you have to do is graft the underarm stitches together. I'm pretty sure I can do it.

I've never made a complete sweater. In high school I started something for my little cousin Gitali in India. I wanted to make a small piece, so I'd have a better chance of finishing. You'd think they wouldn't really wear sweaters in India, but in Bangalore, where my relatives live, it does get chilly sometimes. They want things that wash easily, so Mom took me to K-mart, and we bought some acrylic yarn. Even though it was a small sweater, I never did finish it. Mom had to knit the sleeves and sew it all together.

This yarn is bulky, even thicker than a worsted-weight yarn. I wanted a bulky yarn so it wouldn't take too long to knit up. My mother has patience to work with very thin yarn. I don't have so much patience. At least, that's what she always told me.

And these knitting needles—natural too, except for the plastic wire connecting the bamboo tips. I bought these from the wool woman. Mom always uses straight aluminum needles.

I learned a new cast-on method from this book. The way my mother taught me is, you insert the needle into the previous loop, pull yarn through to make a new loop, and put that loop on the needle. With this method I just learned, you insert the needle *between* the previous two stitches. It makes sense. You don't risk pulling the previous stitch too tight. The author of this book, Elizabeth Zimmerman, is really into loose, relaxed knitting. "Tight knitters lead a hard and anxious life," she says. "If you are a tight knitter by chance instead of by choice, practice knitting loosely, and it may change your life."

My mother's knitting books never included funny philosophical insights.

And maybe there is something to what Elizabeth Zimmerman says. I know I could use some kind of change. I just can't figure out what.

*

I've finished the ribbing and am now into the body of the sweater. I thought I might knit the body plain, in stockinette stitch, until I got to the yoke, but that's too boring. I'm putting in three cables each on the front and back of the sweater. Mom taught me how to do cables.

I haven't been studying for my GMAT. I haven't replied to Josh's texts. He's been calling me, too—my phone sure does ring a lot—but I haven't been answering it or listening to his messages.

I've just been sitting here and knitting. At least I do have an air-conditioner in the window of this room. I can get into the rhythm of the knitting: insert needle, wrap yarn, pull through, slip loop off. Insert, wrap, pull, slip. It's mindless, but it keeps me occupied. Every once in a while, I get to twist the cable stitches.

I need to keep myself occupied. When I'm not knitting or working, I start to panic. It's like I'm jumping into a void or falling into darkness. The knitting helps me stay in the here and now. Nothing matters except the stitches and the yarn slipping through my fingers.

One of my earliest memories is of Mom doing embroidery. I was about five, and we still lived in an apartment. Mom collected embroidery designs—birds, flowers, butterflies. She traced them from magazine pictures, I think. I don't remember how she transferred the designs onto the cloth. Maybe she used carbon paper. It seems to me that she was always engaged in this mysterious, beautiful art, but now I can't even recall what she made. Did she embroider on a shawl, or on a sari?

I remember pestering her to teach me embroidery. She thought I was too young, but I kept after her. One day, Mom sat me down on the big bed in her bedroom. She held a needle threaded with red embroidery floss, already knotted at the end, and a piece of white cloth. She showed me how make a running stitch. I did that for a few minutes, and got bored. It wasn't pretty. So, she taught me the daisy petal chain.

I loved sitting on the bed with my mother, watching her tapered fingers with rounded fingernails maneuver the needle in and out of the cloth. She was beautiful, with creamy brown skin and thick black hair coiled at the back of her head. I always had scabs on my knees, and I screamed every time she tried to cut my nails or clean inside my ears.

Mom gave me back the needle and cloth, and I drew the thread up through the cloth and made a loop, as she had showed me. I carefully slid the needle down again close to the first hole and made it surface farther along, so the needle lay on top of the loop of thread. Then I pulled and hoped that I made a little daisy petal. Mom's fingers hovered over mine, arranging the thread and needle when I failed to get it just right.

"Keep your stitches small and even," Mom reminded me.

She went off to the kitchen or somewhere else. I was all alone in the room. I sat on the bed and made petals for the chain. The gold and brown clock ticked on the nightstand.

After a while I must have gotten bored. I started to poke the needle under the top layer of my skin. I was able to make many tiny tunnels of skin with no bleeding or pain whatsoever. I was fascinated.

Mom walked into the room. I showed her my palm. She scolded me and took the needle away.

"But it doesn't hurt!" I said.

"It is disgusting," she said.

I didn't know why she wasn't more impressed. I had made a scientific discovery: that the top layer of skin is basically dead. But Mom didn't care.

*

I've been thinking—what *is* a good person? What is it that I'm supposed to be doing?

I'm knitting one of the sleeves now. The stitches are on three short double-pointed needles, and I'm using the fourth needle to actually knit with. I hate working with double-pointed needles. There are so many opportunities for stitches to get dropped. I'm working fast now, just wanting to increase enough to transfer the stitches to my shortest circular needle.

When I was a kid, I used to read all these comic books about Hindu mythology. Most of the stories were about boys and men: Rama and Krishna and the Pandava brothers. The women—Sita and Draupadi and Savitri—were beautiful and obedient and cared only for their husbands, never for themselves. Unless they were evil, that is. Kaikeyi was jealous and forced her husband to send Rama into the forest.

So of course, I can't follow those examples.

In elementary school, we learned about Amelia Earhart and Shirley Chisholm and all sorts of strong women who followed their dream, didn't give up, and all of that.

The problem is, I don't have a dream.

I should probably start studying for the GMAT, since summer is about halfway over already.

Even though I hate double-pointed needles, at least I am knitting in the round. I'm doing plain stockinette stitch to get this part over with fast, and it's all knitting, no purling, which is pleasant.

Mom taught me to knit when I was maybe ten. I remember being very frustrated by the whole thing. There were so many loops on the needle, so many stitches that could be dropped by accident. And I was always dropping stitches. Mom would have to take my knitting and use a crochet hook to bring the stitch back up, if it ran down. She'd frown and say, "You are too careless."

Now I can see the beauty of knitting. A knitted fabric is very stretchy but not too thick. Crochet tends to be lumpy and not particularly stretchy.

My mother has never been happy with me. It wasn't just the knitting—I was always careless. I'm too messy, too impatient, too disobedient. My grades aren't good enough. I don't study hard enough. I don't pluck between my eyebrows, I don't sweep under my bed, I forget to return library books on time, I don't always remember to take my shoes off when I come into the house. "It should be automatic!" Mom says. "When you come in the house, the first thing you do is take your shoes off. How many times do you have to be reminded?" I don't know. I just forget. I guess I'm thinking of something else when I walk in the house.

Also, I have no interest in learning how to cook Indian

food. I have no interest in learning how to wrap a sari. I went and attached myself to a white boy and I am allowing him to distract me from my studies.

She's probably right. I am all the things she says. It's my own fault that I have this kind of boring job and dull life and a boyfriend who leaves and then pesters me with texts and phone calls. Last week Josh started threatening to come down and visit me. Yesterday I sent him a nice long chatty e-mail, telling him all sorts of funny stories about work and my housemates: how my fat supervisor eats a sandwich at the beginning of the evening shift and then goes around with a blob of mayonnaise in the corner of her mouth for the rest of the shift; how my housemate of the black plastic walls got upset because another housemate took some the bags off his wall to use for trash during a party. It is all funny when you think about it. Which I try not to do. So anyway, Josh calmed down.

When I'm not knitting or working, my mind thinks bad thoughts about myself. I hate you, I say to myself. You're disgusting.

It's like I'm psychotic or something. I'm not. I'm really normal. I'm so normal, I'm boring. I can't figure out why my mind does this to me.

*

My mother hates me. That's it. I've finally figured out why my mind says these things to me. It's because my mother hates me, and finds me disgusting, and my mind has sort of taken over, since Mom's not here to disapprove of me in person.

Isn't that weird? Isn't that sad? I'm not even *with* my mother, but I've brought my mother's voice with me.

I've finished one sleeve up to the underarm, and I'm furiously working on the other sleeve. I can't wait to put all these stitches onto one big circular needle and start on the yoke. I'm going to use color-stranding to create patterns in the yoke. I have some bright red yarn that'll show up really well against the tan. Mom never taught me this. She never likes to do color-stranding. But that's because the only color-stranding she ever did was this incredibly complicated design: She once made a sweater where it looked like the roses had been painted on. I can't imagine even trying something like that. I'm just going to do some very basic designs that don't require me to carry the other color of yarn for more than a few stitches at a time.

I've got to start studying for my GMAT. Dad has been e-mailing me, asking me how it's going. Fortunately, Dad doesn't expect long e-mails like Josh does, so I can get away with saying something vague like, "Everything is fine here. The weather is hot. Say hi to Mom."

I really am lazy, just like Mom says. I opened my GMAT book the other day, and I read the introduction for the tenth time. But I couldn't motivate myself to do any of the exercises.

I only have one more month of freedom. Of hibernation. Then Josh will be back, and school will start again, and I'll have to perform again.

*

I'm learning to knit the German way. My mother taught me the English method of knitting, where you hold the yarn in your right hand and wrap it around the right-hand needle. In the German method, you hold the yarn in your left hand, and sort of scoop up the yarn with your right needle. This book I have recommends that you learn both ways, so that when you do color-stranding, you can hold a color in each hand.

I like the German method. It's much more ergonomic, it seems to me. Your hands don't move as much.

After I put all the stitches on the large circular needle, I worked about an inch of stockinette stitch, and then started a very simple color pattern: one red stitch, three tan stitches. I'm able to carry the red yarn loosely behind the other stitches. I stopped doing the cables, and they look like they just petered out. Maybe I ought to have knitted a border of garter stitch or something to demarcate their ending. But I'm not going to rip it out now. Mom rips her things out until she gets them perfect. Well, this is not going to be a perfect sweater, but it'll be good enough for me, I guess.

Only three more weeks left until school starts. Even the knitting isn't calming me down now. What am I going to do?

*

I studied for my GMAT. Yesterday I did one entire verbal section from the workbook. The book advises you to study your weakest subject first, which would be math for me, but I thought I'd start slow and do verbal, which is my best subject. Today I'm going to do a math section. I really am.

But first I want to work on this yoke. I'm almost done with this sweater. Can you believe it? Me, almost finished with a sweater? Of course, the yarn is very bulky. That helps. I could never have finished a sweater in thin yarn.

Now I'm putting in some crescent-moon designs that I graphed out. I've already done a design based on my initial, N, which ended up looking like a bunch of slanted mountains because I joined all the N's together. It's fine, though. I knit a row of red in between each pattern. It looks nice. It actually does look nice.

*

I can't do it. I really can't. I feel sick whenever I try to study. Getting an MBA isn't the right thing for me to do. Studying business isn't the right thing for me to do. I'm going home this weekend and telling Mom and Dad that I'm dropping out of college.

The sweater is basically finished. I still have to graft the underarm stitches, but I tried it on, and it fits.

*

I'm at home now. I just drove into the driveway about half an hour ago. I haven't told my parents anything yet. I want to show Mom my sweater first.

When I come downstairs with the sweater, Mom's sitting on a dining chair next to the bright family room window, with a needlepoint frame on a floor stand in front of her. She hardly looks older than she did when I was a kid—her skin is still smooth, her hair is still black (although now from a bottle).

"Here's the sweater I made!" I say, trying to sound enthusiastic and cheerful. Mom often complains that I sulk.

She carefully turns her knees out from under the needlepoint frame before standing up. She holds the sweater by the shoulders and looks at it in the light from the window. She's taller than me, and standing next to her, I still feel like a scrawny child.

"It turned out better than I thought it would," she says.

I glance at her needlepoint. She's covered about half the canvas already. It's so delicate—an intricate floral design leaving no white canvas visible. My sweater looks rough and clunky next to her beautiful work.

Still, I'm proud of my sweater. "It has no seams," I point out. "Look. No sewing." I show her the sides of the sweater where the seams would have been.

"You made it in the round," she says. "I have never used circular needles." She examines the sleeves and shoulders. "How did you attach everything? Are there really no seams?"

I explain how it all worked and show her the grafted underarm stitches. "This is the only part I had to attach together."

She runs her finger over the grafted stitches, and then looks at the whole sweater again. "Very nice, Nandini," she says, and hands the sweater back to me.

I have to be satisfied with that. My mother doesn't praise profusely.

*

I'm back at school, and back in my dorm room. My sweater is sitting in my bottom drawer. Every once in a while, I open the drawer to look at it.

I didn't tell my parents I wanted to drop out of school. I did tell them that I didn't want to take the GMAT. They made a fuss, of course, but I said, "A lot of MBA students have work experience before they apply." Which is true. I read it on a web site. So, they agreed that I could put off applying for my MBA.

I might as well finish my degree, especially since I don't have any bright ideas about what else I want to do. I tell myself, anyone who can knit an entire sweater in one summer can definitely finish her business degree.

I told Josh I wanted a break from our relationship. I told him that I really needed to concentrate on finishing my degree. He pouted, but what could he do?

I've joined a study group to keep me motivated.

I can't wait for cold weather so I can wear my sweater.

*

I'm finished! I graduated. I didn't want to bother with the graduation ceremony, but Mom insisted, so I went through with the whole thing, the cap and gown and all of that. My university is so large that the ceremony was held in the stadium. It was a zoo. But at least it's over.

I'm packing my last things now. Mom and Dad took a lot of stuff in their car already. I'll drive home tomorrow. I'm not sure what I'll be doing for the summer. I'll sign up with some temp agencies, I guess. Of course, Mom and Dad want me to do something spectacular, but I haven't had time to plan spectacles. It's enough that I've graduated.

I bought some new yarn from the wool woman. It's a thin sport weight yarn, a lavender color dyed with elderberries, she said. I'm going to make a gansey sweater out of it. Ganseys are traditional seamless sweaters worn on the British Isles. I have a new book that tells exactly how to do it. I know I won't finish the sweater in a summer, since this yarn is much thinner. But that's OK. I need something to keep me occupied, and the longer it takes, the more occupied I'll be.

I set my bag of yarn in a cardboard packing box and pull my sweater out of my drawer. I wore this sweater every day I could, all winter long. I think it brought me luck. I haven't taken it out since the weather got warm. I lay it out on my bed to look at it.

No. Oh, no. It can't be.

I poke at it. Yes. It's a hole. A ragged hole big enough to put my forefinger through. A moth-hole right in the beautiful yoke.

I fold the sweater in half to hide the hole. I unfold it again. There it is. I fold it back.

I sit down on the bed.

It's my fault. I must have put the sweater away dirty. There must have been a bit of food stuck to the yoke. That's why the moth ate it. I'm careless.

I stand up, crumple the sweater into a ball and stuff it into the box with the new yarn. Oh, well. So, I'll never wear it again. So what? At least making it got me through last summer. I'll make a new sweater. It'll be OK. Nothing's perfect. Right?

*

I feel sad as I drive home. I tell myself it's because I've just graduated, and endings are sad. But I know it's because of the hole in my sweater.

When I get home, I start hauling my boxes up to my room. Above my bed I see the needlepoint my mother was working on last summer. It's framed and hanging on the wall. Why is it in this room? I kick off my shoes, climb on my bed and stand on the pillow to look at it.

It's a spiral of flowers, getting smaller and smaller towards the middle, with gorgeous red roses and leaves on the outside, and delicate flowers in the middle. The stitches are so small, I can hardly make them out.

"That is for you," Mom says.

She's standing in the doorway. Her arms are crossed, each hand holding onto the other elbow. "When you admired it so much last summer, I decided to give it to you," she says. "As one of your graduation presents."

"Wow." I look at the picture again. "I love it. But I thought you were going to hang it in the dining room."

"I want you to have it," she says. "Everything I have will be yours one day."

I sit down on the bed. I don't deserve everything Mom has. I'm just a lazy, clumsy girl who leaves food on her sweater for moths to eat.

The box with my sweater is on the floor beside me. I wres-

tle open the top and pull it out. "There's a hole here!" I wail. I
thrust the sweater towards her, and tears burst out of my eyes.
I hope my mother will think I'm just crying about the sweater,
and not about the needlepoint she gave me.

Mom takes the sweater in her hands and examines the hole.
"Did you save the extra yarn?" she asks.

I did. I did save the extra yarn. I dive into the box and tri-
umphantly pull out a plastic bag holding a ball of tan yarn and
a ball of red yarn. "Here."

She takes the bag, her eyes still on my sweater. "I can fix it,"
she says.

I watch her leave the room. I'm not so careless after all. I
saved the yarn.

*

A week later, when I come in after my first day at a temp
job, Mom calls me into the family room. She's sitting in her
favorite spot, by the bright window.

"Here is your sweater." She holds it out to me.

I take it and look at the yoke. Then I turn it around and
look at the yoke on the other side. I turn it back. I can see absolutely no sign of any hole.

"If you look inside, you will see the yarn-ends where I fixed
it."

I peek inside the sweater and see the yarn-ends. "How did
you do it?"

Mom shrugs. "Since you had the exact yarn, I just tried to
match the stitches."

"It's not easy to repair a hole that big."

"It wasn't such a big hole."

"You fixed it so it doesn't show at all. It was a big hole."

"No, Nandini," Mom insists. "It was a small hole, and easy

to fix. You must not get so upset about little things."

Mom has already turned back to the craft magazine she was reading. I fold the bulky sweater over my arm and slowly carry it up the stairs. In front of the mirror above my dresser, I put the sweater on and stroke the section where the hole used to be. My image, in the mirror, strokes her good-as-new sweater too. I can hardly feel the small knots Mom made in the back of the knit fabric, to hold everything together.

MRS. RAGHAVENDRA'S DAUGHTER

Mrs. Raghavendra has discovered the purpose of life. She's sitting at her kitchen table considering her discovery while drinking her afternoon coffee. As she thinks, she presses her fingertip over a mess of crumbs sprinkled on the placemat, which shows a view of Niagara Falls. This placemat was bought back when her husband was alive, back when she still took trips to see tourist attractions.

The crumbs are from the one vanilla cookie she has just eaten, as she does every afternoon. She would have liked to eat a chocolate chip cookie, but three years ago she made a vow to give up chocolate until her daughter, Anjana, got married. She deposits the crumbs into a small pile in one corner of the placemat.

Mrs. Raghavendra has lived alone for the past seven years, ever since Anjana went to college. She still lives in the same tract house that she and her husband built fifteen years ago, with their own choice of carpet colors and wallpaper patterns. Five years after the house was completed, her husband had died. So, Mrs. Raghavendra has no one nearby to whom she can convey her discovery. But this doesn't bother her, because she doesn't plan on telling anyone. Not out of spite, but simply because it doesn't occur to her that anyone would be interested in this thought of hers. After all, who is she to say what the purpose of life is? She's just a cowardly woman whose daughter has reached the age of twenty-five without being married.

Mrs. Raghavendra pushes back her chair, picks up her coffee cup and saucer, and carries them to the sink. Then she opens the cabinet door under the sink, removes a dish rag from a hook on the inside of the door, and walks back to the table, where she wipes the crumbs off the mat. She returns to the sink, rinses the dish rag, and replaces it on the hook. She sighs. It's just 3:00. Her coffee ritual took only fifteen minutes.

What should she do? She's already washed her dirty clothes from her trip to see Anjana. She could watch several craft and garden shows on TV until it is time to cook dinner. Or maybe she won't even make dinner. Maybe she'll just eat some toast and fruit, or a bowl of cereal. Who wants to bother getting out the pots, oil, and spices for just one person?

She sits again at the table, slumped over with her hands in her lap, and stares at the placemat. She would hate to have anyone see her like this—just sitting and staring. But since there is no one to see her, she allows herself to stay in this position. Mrs. Raghavendra sighs. She wonders, again, if she might have caused this—this problem of Anjana's. If her husband were still alive, would that have made the difference? Is it Mrs. Raghavendra's cowardice that has led to this?

No one expected him to die so young. Anjana was only fifteen then. He was a vegetarian, never drank, never smoked, did fifteen minutes of exercises every single day. Still, he died of a heart attack before the age of fifty.

After his death Mrs. Raghavendra spent weeks in hysterics, more because of panic than sadness. How would she ever cope? Her brother in Cleveland, Guru, tried to teach her how to handle the finances and investments, but she couldn't keep anything straight—those piles of statements with lists of numbers on them. She felt really stupid about it. Why couldn't she be cleverly self-sufficient, like so many other women, even Indian women of her own age? Finally, Guru arranged for everything to be sent to his home, so he could handle it.

"What should we do now?" Mrs. Raghavendra asks out loud, sitting at the table. She talks to her husband every day, out of habit. For the first few years after he died, she felt he was still with her, watching over her. She imagined him comforting her, encouraging her, leaning over her as she cried. The biggest question at that point had been, what to do with Anjana? Should Mrs. Raghavendra take her back to India? How would she handle an American teenager all by herself?

But one reason they had settled in the US in the first place was for the American educational system. Her husband had received his PhD in biomechanical engineering from the University of Texas, and he wanted American opportunities for Anjana. She discussed all the possibilities with her brother Guru and her sister Viji in India: Anjana could go to India to finish high school, and then return to the US for college; Anjana could go to India, finish her bachelor's degree and get married, and then return for further education; Anjana could stay in the US but must live at home throughout college. Finally, Mrs. Raghavendra decided they had best stay put for the time being. The house was paid off, the life insurance money was ample, so why uproot themselves? Anyway, these days even girls in India were becoming more and more forward. She told her daughter they would remain in the US if Anjana stayed out of trouble.

"Don't go dating any boys," Mrs. Raghavendra warned. Daily she prayed to Vishnu, Lakshmi, and Ganesha to keep Anjana away from American boys. Perhaps because of the warning, or because of the prayers, Anjana had been a really good, quiet girl in high school. She didn't even pester her mother about going to the senior prom, like so many other Indian girls did.

Then, while Anjana was in college, Mrs. Raghavendra thought about the other big question: what to do about Anjana's marriage? Her husband had often commented that the way to find a match was not through impersonal matrimonial ads, but through "connections." So, Mrs. Raghavendra wrote to all of their relatives in India, and told all of her South Indian friends in the area, especially those of the same sub-caste, that she was looking for a boy for Anjana. Somehow Anjana found out about it. She got so angry—shouting and screaming, when she was normally such a calm girl—that Mrs. Raghavendra had to promise not to pursue it anymore. "I don't want to get married!" Anjana had screamed.

In a way this made perfect sense. After all, what well-bred Indian girl admitted that she wanted to get married? Good girls were shy about that. Mrs. Raghavendra herself had told her parents she didn't want to get married. Her parents had introduced her to a quiet young man, just returned from completing his PhD in America, and she had somehow allowed herself to be led towards matrimony, blushing and stammering all the way.

Maybe some other mothers would have been more daring in the face of a daughter's anger, but Mrs. Raghavendra had always been a softie. A coward.

Anjana graduated from college and moved away from home to attend law school. Now Anjana had her first job as a lawyer, in Washington, DC. Mrs. Raghavendra went to visit her knowing she couldn't wait any longer. She went with a plan. But again, her cowardice got in the way, and now she knows there is nothing more she will do.

On the way home, she was sitting on the plane thinking about her visit, and depending on what part she thought about, she felt alternately extremely embarrassed, or satisfied and peaceful. And at one of the satisfied and peaceful moments, she had her insight about the purpose of life.

*

Anjana was not looking forward to her mother's visit. She couldn't remember the last time she was eager to see her mother, which was really a shame, really pitiful, since she and her mother had only each other. So, this visit was no different. Anjana cleaned up the apartment and hid anything telltale: a brochure about a women-only vacation cruise, rainbow flags, pink triangle pins—although her mother probably had no idea what any of that symbolized—and even her CD collection, filled with k.d. lang and Holly Near and other incriminating people her mother had never heard of.

Susan sat around and didn't help at all. "Don't you think your mom knows by now?" she asked, picking up the *Girl-friends* magazine out of the to-be-recycled pile. "When are you going to come out to her? I mean, we've been together for years. Your mom's no dummy. She's gotta have figured it out."

Anjana snatched the magazine away from Susan and stuffed it back into the bag. "Yeah, we've been together, but we've never lived together before. You don't know my mother as well as I do. She doesn't just figure things out. She's still trying to get me to have an arranged marriage! If my mom found out the truth, she'd die. She'd just die."

So, the apartment was cleaned up. Anjana even thought about setting up the spare room as "Anjana's" room, in which

Mom would be sleeping while Anjana slept on the "floor" of "Susan's" room. But this would have required Anjana to haul everything in the spare room down to the basement storage area, and then to somehow procure bedroom furniture for that room. Anjana transferred some clothes to the closet of the spare room. She thought that, if they just kept both bedroom doors closed, Mom might not notice where they went to sleep at night.

Mrs. Raghavendra arrived on Saturday morning. "Why is your apartment so small?" she asked. "And there are two of you, both lawyers. Doesn't that Susan pay rent?"

"Of course." Anjana put Mom's suitcase in a corner of the living room. She tried to ignore the fact that Mom was still referring to Susan as "that Susan."

"Then?" Mom plumped her large purse beside the suitcase and sat on the sofa. "Why couldn't you get a decent place?"

"We're in a *great* location, Mom," Anjana insisted. "Just a few blocks from Dupont Circle. And we have a balcony, see?" Anjana pointed to a tiny square of concrete outside a sliding glass door.

"OK, great location, but what about this furniture?"

Anjana saw the furniture through her mother's eyes. There was a heavy solid wood coffee table which was, most of the time, covered with papers, books, and mugs. Now that it was clean, the surface revealed several scratches. The brick-and-board bookshelf leaned precariously against the back wall.

"You don't have to live like a student anymore." Mrs. Raghavendra stood up and walked around the apartment. "The carpet looks nice, at least."

Anjana looked down at the tan carpeting, hardly stained at all.

Her mother stood in the hallway. "Two bedrooms, right?"

"Yeah." Anjana rushed to her mother's side and stood

between Mom and the bedroom doors.

"Is this one yours?" Mrs. Raghavendra pointed to the one Anjana was standing nearest.

Anjana waved away the question. "It's really a mess, Mom. I haven't had a chance to decorate it yet. I don't want you to see it now."

Anjana had planned what she thought was a nice outing for that day. She wanted to show her mother something really special in Washington, DC. There was a neat Frida Kahlo exhibit at the National Museum of Women in the Arts, but she didn't think Mom would appreciate surrealistic paintings of a beetle-browed Mexican woman. Instead, she took Mom to the Sackler gallery to look at the ancient Hindu sculptures. Mom was very religious.

*

On Monday morning, Mrs. Raghavendra woke up on the futon sofa in the living room, knowing this was the day she would put her plan into action. She was going to spend the day alone in Anjana's apartment, while Anjana and Susan went to work. Mrs. Raghavendra couldn't take the subway anywhere. She was too afraid. And there wasn't much to walk to around Anjana's house—just various stores and restaurants. So, it was the perfect time to do what she meant to do.

The girls didn't even eat breakfast, not even cereal. "We'll get a muffin on the way," they called as they whisked around the apartment, putting on suit-jackets and pumps and picking up briefcases. Mrs. Raghavendra sat at the breakfast bar drinking her coffee, trying to stay out of their way. She noticed that Anjana kept going in and out of her bedroom, and then Susan's bedroom, and then her bedroom.

As soon as she heard the key turn in the lock, Mrs. Raghavendra's mind began working on her plan, although she continued to sit. She listened to the girls' heels clicking smartly down the apartment building's hallway, loud and then more and more faintly, until she couldn't hear them anymore. Then she went into the bathroom to take her shower. There, on the floor of the bathroom, she noticed Susan's T-shirt—the one she had been wearing the day before—and bra. She stared at the clothes, cradling her toiletries pouch. Anjana was making good money. Why did she have to have a roommate? Anjana and Susan had gone to law school together, and had both, coincidentally, found jobs in Washington, DC. Didn't that Susan have any other friends to live with? And what about these boyfriends that American girls were always running after? Of course, Susan's mother probably didn't care whether Susan ever got married. Mrs. Raghavendra knew these Americans didn't trouble themselves to find spouses for their children.

She set Susan's clothes on the bathroom counter and finished her shower.

It was time. She had already noticed where it was—the thing she needed for her plan. She sat on the edge of the sofa and looked at it, slumped on one of the lower shelves of the bookshelf, so fat and heavy that she wondered if she should scrap her plan. "Are you going to be a coward all your life?" she asked herself silently.

She stood up and walked past the sliding door that led to the tiny balcony. Someone had taken the time to plant marigolds in the little flower box, and the view was nice—the apartment was high enough that she looked out among the treetops. There were two white plastic chairs on the balcony. Should she go out there and sit down for a while?

No. She must continue with her plan. She reached the bookshelf, lifted the phone book, and pulled her phone out of her purse. She dropped the heavy, floppy book up on the breakfast bar and settled herself on one of the tall stools. She felt a familiar fretful worry in her heart, like some sharp-clawed beast trying to escape its cage, but she barred the door tight and turned away. This phone book was so huge, much thicker than the normal-sized directory she used at home. Although she had a smart phone, she'd never figured out how to do much with it.

Mrs. Raghavendra resolutely opened the book and started paging through it, to keep her mind off her worry. After all, she had to do *something*.

The bra. Mrs. Raghavendra couldn't stop herself thinking about it lying there on the bathroom floor like a pile of used napkins. That was what made Mrs. Raghavendra's worry surface again, sniffing and gnawing at the bars of its cage. It reminded her of the time she had found a stray bra—clearly not Anjana's, it was much too large—among Anjana's laundry. Standing in the basement laundry room, holding the too-large bra, Mrs. Raghavendra's heart had been struck with horror. A bolt of lightning flashed on a monster in the previously safe darkness. What was going on with Anjana?

That day in the basement, Mrs. Raghavendra had tried to shake the suspicion out of her head. How silly. What could be more natural than two roommates getting their clothes mixed up? Mrs. Raghavendra quickly slammed the door on the monster, but still she had stood there, immobile with fear. Maybe her prayers had been a little too effective. Could she take them back? Maybe a white man for Anjana would not be as bad as— as *this*.

Sitting at the dining bar, Mrs. Raghavendra shook her head. She knew she must erase her mind of such thoughts. And about her own daughter, too! There was nothing in the cage. Nothing at all. She was just imagining things. She heaved herself off her chair, hurried into the bathroom, plucked the bra from the counter with the tips of her thumb and forefinger, opened Susan's bedroom door an inch, and threw it in. Susan was just a messy girl, that's all.

In front of the phone book again, Mrs. Raghavendra sent up a short, silent prayer to—to whom? Which God could help Anjana with her problem—if it was a problem? Would it be Krishna, the handsome cowherd who made all the girls swoon? Would it be Manmatha, the God of love? No one had ever talked about love when Mrs. Raghavendra was growing up.

But maybe Mrs. Raghavendra was reading too much into everything. How was she to know what was what in this strange country where girls and boys kissed openly, but men were not supposed to hold hands with men, and women were not supposed to hold hands with women, and then everyone did God only knew what behind closed doors? If only he had lived, he would have known what to do. He would not have given in to Anjana's anger so readily. He would not have been such a coward. And Anjana would have been safely married by now.

"Susan and your other friends will get married someday," Mrs. Raghavendra sometimes pointed out to Anjana. "They will not have so much time to spend with you. And then what will you do?" But Anjana only smiled. "Don't worry about me, Mom."

Occasionally Mrs. Raghavendra was tempted to take this advice—to let Anjana find her own husband. After all, she was an American girl. She could take care of herself. Then she would see a vision of Anjana, old and gray-haired, living alone among piles of dusty law books. Sometimes, distressingly, a gigantic white bra would suddenly appear, draped over one of the books.

Perhaps a bolder woman would not worry like this about a grown daughter. A brave woman would not sit all day in a tiny apartment in Washington, DC, poring over the phone book.

Yesterday, Sunday, Anjana had tried to teach Mrs. Raghavendra how to use the subway system. "It's easy, Mom," she insisted. "You just take the red line to this stop here"—she pointed to a tiny circle on a map full of tangled colored lines—"then transfer to the orange or blue lines and ride it to the Smithsonian stop. You can go to any museum on the Mall while I'm at work."

Mrs. Raghavendra knew she'd never bother to go that far underground and try to take a train somewhere all by herself, even if she had wanted to go to a museum.

She looked down at the phone book again. She placed a fingertip at the top of the "A" column and began scanning down the names. This is what she had to do. Her good friend Kanta Lakshman told her that whenever she was in a new city, she looked up South Indian names in the phone book and called someone to find out where the Hindu temple was, and whether there were any good Indian vegetarian restaurants nearby. Mrs. Raghavendra was going just one step further, using the phone book to find a son-in-law. If only Anjana could meet the right man, she might agree to be married. But how would she ever meet a South Indian man in this big city full of white and black people? She worked all the time and didn't even go to the Hindu temple. The only way was for Mrs. Raghavendra to find the man for her.

Two hours later, she had come up with a list of likely names and phone numbers. Now she would begin. But first, she eased herself off the stool and slowly stretched her cramped arms over her head. She took her coffee cup to the sink, soaped it, rinsed it, dried it, and put it away. She glanced around the apartment and saw the drooping philodendron on the bookshelf. She opened a cabinet, got out a glass, and filled it from the filtered-water spigot.

As she passed by her phone list on the way to the philodendron, she stopped. "Don't be such a coward," she whispered out loud. She set the glass down and picked up the phone. She took a few deep breaths and, without even sitting down, started dialing. Mrs. Raghavendra didn't know what she would say when someone answered the phone. She just kept repeating "om namo narayanaya" in the back of her mind as she listened to the phone ringing on the other end. God would put the right words into her mouth when the time came.

She got voice mail on the first couple of calls. She hung up without leaving messages. She set the phone down. A single Indian man would be busy at work during the day. He would be in meetings and so forth and could not answer his phone. What was she thinking? But she couldn't wait until evening because Anjana would be home then. She must not give up now. Maybe by chance someone would answer. She climbed up onto the stool, picked up the phone again and dialed.

"Hello?" It was a man's voice.

"Hello?" Mrs. Raghavendra whispered.

"Hello?"

"Yes. Hello." She swallowed. She waited a few seconds.

"Hello?" the man said again.

Mrs. Raghavendra found that, after all, she had nothing to say. So, while the man on the other end continued to shout "Hello," Mrs. Raghavendra took the phone from her ear and, very gently, touched the red "hang up" button. Then she set the phone on the dining bar.

She sat there for many minutes. Then she slid down off the seat. She almost fell, the seat was so high, and she was so short. Stowing the phone in her purse, she heaved the phone book into her arms and stuffed it back on the bookshelf. She picked up the glass of water, stepped over to the philodendron, and carefully tipped water around its roots. "Now you will feel better," she murmured to the plant. Even though she was a coward, at least she could be a useful coward.

As she watered the plant, her gaze was drawn to the bedroom doors. Which one was Susan's? Or, did they both—? She looked away, but it was no use. She heard the monster again, pacing in its cage. The beast pawed and whined, looking towards the bedroom doors, as though it wanted to go in.

Suddenly, Mrs. Raghavendra turned. She strode forward and put her hand on a doorknob. Then she shut her eyes and threw the door open. Slowly she lifted her eyelids. She and the beast both stared, breathless. Anjana was right—the room was a mess. Mrs. Raghavendra could see two bikes, stacks of dusty cardboard boxes, and two sets of skis. There wasn't even any bed. How could Anjana sleep here?

Mrs. Raghavendra closed the door and stepped to the next one, pushing it open silently.

A large bed. Just one. It was made up neatly. In India, it might have been unremarkable for two girls sharing an apartment to share a bedroom, perhaps even a bed if space was tight. But in the US?

The entire bedroom was done in black and white, with no lace in sight. Anjana had never loved the bright colors her mother favored. The bedspread was plain and gray. A black and white striped rug lay on the shiny wood floor. White vertical blinds shaded the window. On the wall, a large Indian batik in shades of tan and brown showed two village women, one arranging the other's hair.

The only spots of color were in the photographs on the sleek black dresser. In one, twelve-year-old Anjana in a lacy dress—perhaps the last time she let her mother dress her for a picture—stood with an arm around each of her seated parents, her father in a dark suit and her mother in a bright green and yellow sari. Mrs. Raghavendra picked up the frame and peered at Anjana's sweet childhood face. Anjana had been hers then.

She turned to the other photograph on the dresser, Anjana in the black robe of a scholar, hugging Susan at their law school graduation. Could Mrs. Raghavendra have really given birth to this grown-up stranger?

The room was much neater than Mrs. Raghavendra had expected. Really, the only thing messy was the bra which she herself had thrown in there. Mrs. Raghavendra stooped down, picked up the bra, and folded it in her hands.

The creature was still but alert—she could hear its even breathing. Absently, she rubbed the soft satin of the bra under one palm, as though stroking the creature's fur. It was surprisingly silky. The creature sighed and closed its eyes. Mrs. Raghavendra tiptoed over to the dresser and placed the bra next to the graduation picture. She backed out of the bedroom and softly closed the door, leaving the creature sleeping soundly inside.

*

That evening, the girls came home to a hot meal, and the three of them sat eating in the living room. For the first time, Mrs. Raghavendra looked at Susan—really looked at her. She was a tall, well-built girl. Her skin was very fair, but unfortunately it was pocked all over with brown freckles. Her hair was a reddish-yellow color, as were her eyebrows and eyelashes, so her face seemed naked. Her eyes were a pale blue, and her lips mere outlines around her mouth. Too bad she was so ugly. That was the problem with fair-skinned people. Along with the nice white skin came colorless hair and eyes. Anjana, on the other hand—Mrs. Raghavendra turned to look at her daughter—was just perfect. Slim, and not too dark. She had their family's coffee-with-cream complexion. Her large black eyes were rimmed with long lashes and accented with thick brows, and her lips were full and brown.

Susan's ugliness didn't seem to bother Susan at all. She was very friendly, ate a lot of food, and didn't complain of the spiciness. At one point, she told a story about someone in her office, a very pompous man from what Mrs. Raghavendra gathered, and the story involved a word that Mrs. Raghavendra had never heard before.

"What does that mean?" she asked.

Anjana and Susan looked at each other. Anjana shrugged and gazed down at her plate.

Then Susan turned to Mrs. Raghavendra and explained, "It means to pass wind."

Mrs. Raghavendra still looked puzzled, so Susan put her lips on her broad white forearm and gave an audible demonstration, after which she pointed theatrically at her rear end while winking.

"Oh?" Fart. Mrs. Raghavendra smiled. Fart. It was such a perfect word. And that Susan—how she explained it! She looked at Susan and started to laugh. Susan began chuckling, and every time they looked at each other, they laughed harder. Mrs. Raghavendra had to put her water cup down so she wouldn't spill it.

Mrs. Raghavendra wiped her eyes and Susan threw herself back against the sofa, clutching her belly. They both looked at Anjana. Mrs. Raghavendra noticed that her daughter seemed bewildered. She seemed almost on the verge of tears.

*

It is growing dark outside the kitchen window. Sitting at the table for so long, lost in thought, Mrs. Raghavendra didn't even notice the setting sun. Anjana might be home from work by now. She really should get up and call her daughter, at least to report her safe arrival home. But she makes no move to get the phone out of her purse. The purpose of life—it came to her as the flight attendant handed her a cup of ginger ale, and she was so startled, she almost dropped the flimsy plastic cup.

What is the purpose of life? Nothing more, nor less, than this: to teach us to get along with each other, and to help each other. That's why God made it so hard, so that we would have to work at it. That's why God made Anjana the way she is, and made Mrs. Raghavendra afraid of that way, so Mrs. Raghavendra would have to see through this fear to the truth. On the airplane, Mrs. Raghavendra thought she could do it. She could allow Anjana to be who she is, and it wouldn't matter what anyone—her friends, the relatives in India—said or thought.

Should she tell Anjana her discovery? Maybe it's better not to say anything at all. She doesn't want to embarrass her daughter. But she can't just sit here all evening. She puts her palms on the table, heaves herself up, finds her purse, and extracts the phone. Tomorrow when she goes to the Indian grocery for her weekly shopping, she'll buy one of those chocolate bars with the raisins and nuts—her favorite.

*

When Anjana hears her phone ring, she is transferring her clothes from the spare room back to the bedroom closet. She feels guilty about her mother's visit. She thinks her mother must know. First of all, after her mother left, Susan told her that someone—her mother it must have been, who else was in the apartment that day? —someone had folded Susan's bra and put it on the dresser. If so, her mother has been in the bedroom. If so, her mother knows. Or does she? Is Mom perceptive enough to guess?

Mom was so nice to Susan that evening. Anjana remembers

their laughter. Their faces glowed. Her mother's eyes were like those of a little girl, open and fresh. At that moment, Anjana wanted to throw her arms around her mother, bury her face in her neck, and cry and cry. Instead she swallowed and pressed her napkin to her lips.

She feels she has treated her mother badly. She cannot please her mother by doing things her own way—by landing a prestigious job, living in a hip area of town, taking her mother to museums. Sometimes she wishes she could be the kind of daughter her mother wants, marrying a nice Indian man and providing grandchildren. It would be so much easier.

Anjana looks at the screen on her phone. It is her mother. "Hello?"

"Hello, raja. I just wanted to call and say that I reached here safely."

Anjana feels a tightening around her heart, as she always does when she hears or sees her mother. "That's good. Was the flight OK?" She stands by the kitchen counter, scraping her fingernail at a splotch of something.

"Yes, fine. I hope I didn't inconvenience you too much."

"Oh, no, of course not, Mom." Anjana shakes her head vigorously to add intensity where truth is lacking. "I wish you had been able to do more, though."

"I was fine."

"Well, it was nice to see you."

"OK, then, I'll let you go."

"Bye, Mom."

Pause. Neither of them hangs up. Anjana doesn't want to give the impression that she can't wait to get off the phone with her mother. She can hear her mother breathing on the other end.

"OK, then," her mother says again. "Say hi to Susan."

An electric shock shoots through Anjana's heart. What

does it *mean* that her mother wants her to say hi to Susan all of a sudden? Or does it mean anything at all? Maybe she's reading too much into things. Finally, she says, "Sure, Mom."

Anjana puts the phone down and turns to look out the sliding glass door. She flips the latch on the door, pulls it open, and steps out into the summer evening. The heat of the day has started to dissipate. She stands at the edge of the balcony, looking down at the street. The apartment is on the fifth floor and, although she's never been afraid of heights before, she feels a little vertigo, as though she might find herself falling over the balcony railing. She shifts her eyes up, over the treetops, and realizes it's only that she feels buoyant. She might float up into the air like a helium balloon.

CRYSTAL VASE: SNAPSHOTS

Revati stumbled as she entered the back door of her newly renovated kitchen-dining area clutching the thick stems of ivory tulips. The screen door clicked shut and she stopped to take a breath. The kitchen was redolent with the scent of baking cheese and garlic from the lasagna in the oven. Her husband, Bernard, ripped romaine lettuce at the counter.

"Hold these while I fill up the vase." She thrust the flowers at him.

He accepted the stems. "Calm down."

"I am calm." She climbed a stool to reach the cabinet above the fridge.

"I'm ready, Mommy." Her five-year-old daughter appeared at her side.

"You might be hot in that velvet dress." Revati stepped down with a tall, sleek rectangular glass vase pressed to her chest.

"I want to look beautiful for your friend Liz."

*

Revati turned the page of the photo album. "I remember taking this one in her bedroom, right before we went to a Girl Scout meeting." The background of the square Polaroid was almost black, and Liz's white face glowed like a ghost. She sat on her bed in a white blouse and pleated green skirt, her Girl Scout sash draped over her chest.

Bernard pointed to a mound of something on the bed behind Liz.

Revati leaned over the picture. "There were always piles of clothes everywhere. Sometimes she wouldn't know if they were dirty or clean."

"Sounds unpleasant," Bernard said.

Revati raised her eyes from the album. "It was a wonderful place. We could do anything we wanted, and no one got upset. We'd eat things I wasn't allowed to at home. Cherry pie filling. We'd squirt whipped cream from a can all over it."

"I want to eat some!" Arsha ran to the refrigerator.

"Fortunately, we don't have any cherry pie filling." Bernard spooned Dijon mustard into a salad-dressing bottle, and added a stream of gold olive oil. "Sounds like her parents neglected her."

"No, Bernard. It was a cheerful house."

Bernard shook the dressing bottle vigorously. "Cheerful in what way?"

*

Liz left the next morning after brunch. "I've got an early shift Monday," she explained. "You have such a nice family,

Revati. I'll be really lonely now."

"You don't have to be lonely." Revati tried to be cheerful and reassuring. "Call me anytime."

"I'll send you the pictures," she said.

Liz didn't send the promised selfies they'd taken with her phone, but Revati received two text messages right away. The first one thanked her for the visit. The other message asked, "What does a person do with nothing to live four"

Revati, late for a meeting, couldn't help cringing at the wrong word use and lack of punctuation. She tapped quickly, "You sound desperate. Is that true?"

Almost immediately, Liz replied: "Not going to kill myself or anything"

*

"She moved away when we were in sixth grade."

"So . . . about thirty years ago? What made her contact you all of a sudden?"

"She said she was looking for people from her past. She was looking for *me*, Bernard. She said I was the best friend she ever had." Revati held out her hands for the tulips and began trimming the stems.

"And . . . you invited her for the entire weekend."

"She's driving down all the way from Ohio."

"You could've just visited with her when you went up to see your parents."

"She's never been to DC before. I felt like she needed a vacation. You didn't have to leave work early today if you didn't want to." She adjusted the tulips in the water, so the taller ones were in the center.

"I don't mind. It's just that I don't get why she's so important. You've never mentioned her before."

"We'd just arrived from India, and she was my first friend, back when other kids were put off by my accent." She set the tulips in their vase on the dining table. "I'll show you a picture of Liz."

*

As Revati changed her clothes upstairs, the doorbell rang. "I'll get it!" Arsha screamed, running to the door.

"Look out the window and make sure it's Liz," Revati called, hurrying down. Arsha hadn't yet opened the door.

"Who is it?" Revati asked.

"Some old lady," she whispered.

Revati pushed aside the curtain on the door. Standing on the porch was a heavy-set, middle-aged woman with short graying hair, wearing a black jacket and jeans and carrying a large white shopping bag. Her face broke into a smile and Revati recognized, in the crooked teeth and crinkled eyes, something of her friend from long ago.

Before she opened the door, Revati bent to her daughter's ear. "Don't say that. Liz is not old," she murmured. "She's the same age as Mommy."

*

"On weekends her dad would sit in front of the TV watching *The Three Stooges* and drinking beer, and he'd laugh and laugh. Her mom had all these clothes from when she used to be thin, lingerie and cocktail dresses and high heels. Liz and I would go down to the basement and try them on and do fashion shows for each other."

Bernard lifted an eyebrow. "Two ten-year-old girls modeling lingerie for each other?"

"What's lonjeray?" Arsha wanted to know.

"Bernard, it wasn't like that."

"What is it?" Arsha asked again.

"Nothing, sweetie. What I'm trying to say, Bernard, is that Liz's house was so different from mine."

"What're you getting so excited about?" he asked.

Revati lowered her voice. "Sorry. But do you get it? At my house, I never put a picture on the wall of my room without asking Mom first, and she'd usually say no because she didn't want to ruin the paint. The walls of Liz's room were plastered with posters and photos of her favorite musicians. She loved Michael Jackson. Madonna was getting popular. Liz told me which radio stations to listen to. We watched music videos and practiced moon walking."

"If you were such good friends, why'd you stop being friends?"

"She moved away." Revati shrugged. "Her dad left the family," she said to the photos in her arms. "Liz's mom moved everyone down to southern Ohio, to live with her mother. That was in the spring of sixth grade."

"So, you could never play with her again?" Arsha's forehead wrinkled with worry.

Revati stroked her daughter's head. "At first we wrote a lot. And then . . ." her gaze drifted back to the photos. "My parents bought a house in a new subdivision in Kent, and in the fall, I started seventh grade. I made new friends. I fit in with the other girls because of everything Liz had taught me."

"And you stopped writing," Bernard said.

"I remember her last letter at the beginning of seventh grade. She said her dad was having a baby with his girlfriend. She said her parents were getting a divorce." Looking up from the album, she quirked the corners of her mouth into a smile for Arsha. "She said her dad brought her a puppy. And you know what, Arsha?"

"What?" Arsha asked breathlessly.

"She named her dog 'Revati.' I bet you didn't know that I had a dog named after me."

*

"You haven't changed a bit," Liz exclaimed, stepping inside and enveloping Revati in a hug, just as Liz's mother used to. "You're still slim. You've still got that beautiful shiny black hair I used to love so much. You could pass for twenty-five, Revati. Really, you could." She set down the large white paper bag and struggled out of her jacket.

Revati accepted the jacket. "That's a pretty sweater," she offered in exchange. Liz wore a bulky top festooned with cables and bobbles.

"Thank you. Purple's my favorite color." Liz walked into the living room. "You have a beautiful house. I love wood floors. And good light from all the windows. When I heard you lived in a row house, I thought it would be dark."

"We're lucky to have a corner house," Revati agreed.

Liz craned her neck at the bookshelves. "Lots of books. I remember you were reading that *Little Women* series and every day at the bus stop you'd tell me the story, word for word."

"That must have been annoying."

"It was!" She broke into a peal of laughter. "I only put up with it because I loved you. Oh, I almost forgot." She lugged over the big white bag and lifted a large box out of it. "I thought you might like this."

*

"Yes, thank you, Revati," Liz said. "I did receive them."

"Have you looked at them?"

"Haven't had a chance yet. I'm not a big reader, you know."

"Let me know if I can help in any way."

Revati didn't hear from Liz after that. She texted but got no reply. In a few days, Revati called her once more, and again Liz insisted she was "not so bad" and that she had not had a chance to look at the books or to call a counselor.

"Liz, I'm worried about you. Keep in touch, will you?"

"Sure."

"Call me anytime."

"Sure."

Revati waited for the phone to go silent before hanging up. She continued to hear Liz huffing.

"Are you still there, Liz?"

"You know, Revati, I thought—" She paused.

"Yes?"

"I thought about you so much when I was growing up in Marietta. Our friendship was the happiest thing I could remember. When I saw you again, I thought maybe I could—I don't know—capture that happiness again." She paused. "You can never go back again, can you?"

*

At dinner, Liz ate slowly, chewing carefully and patting her lips with her napkin. She refused the wine Bernard offered. "I'm not much of a drinker," she said. "I wouldn't know a good wine from vinegar." Then she gave a short, deep chuckle. She sounded just like her mother. "Anyway, seeing the damage alcohol did to my family, I decided early on to avoid the stuff."

Revati felt Bernard's glance on her. How had she not realized that alcohol was a problem in Liz's family?

After a moment Revati asked Liz about her mother and younger sisters.

"Since I moved back up north, I don't talk to them much anymore. I'm not really welcome at home." Liz poked a leaf of lettuce with her fork and placed it carefully in her mouth.

"Why not?" Revati asked.

She broke open a dinner roll and buttered it slowly. "I guess it was about three years ago," she said. "I was still living in Marietta. I was working at the hardware store and I had my own place. One day, out of the blue, Dad calls. He must've found me through directory assistance, because I certainly never tried to contact him. I hadn't seen him since he brought down my puppy. Mom was so depressed after the divorce and I sided with her.

"So, as I said, Dad calls. He says he's sick, he has liver cancer, he has no one to take care of him. 'What about your wife?' I ask. Well, it turned out she'd left him. So, there he was, all alone up there in the hospital. He asks me to come up and see him. 'I know I haven't been a good father,' he says. 'Can you forgive me?'

"I felt sorry for him. For a couple years I was actually thinking I might want to try to find my Dad's other kids—my half-siblings. I didn't even know how many kids he had, or anything. I thought, that's no way to live, to not even know my own blood relations. I told my mom and sisters that I was going up north to see Dad, and they just about blew a fuse." Liz used her fork to drag pieces of arugula to the edge of her plate.

*

"She was ten in this picture." The girl stood with hands resting on a wooden "fence" in front of a meadow scene. "All our school pictures that year had this same fence and backdrop."

Bernard stood behind Revati, arms around her waist and chin resting on her shoulder. "She doesn't look too happy."

"What d'you mean?" She elbowed him away.

*

She didn't know where to put the vase Liz had given her. A week after Liz's visit, it still sat on the coffee table in the middle of the living room. "It's so big and awkward," she told Bernard that night as they relaxed on the sofa with glasses of wine. She eyed the bulging vase encrusted with embellishments. "It won't fit on the fireplace mantle. If I leave it on that table, Arsha might knock it over."

"Do you like it?"

"It's way too fussy."

"Donate it to Goodwill, then."

"But Liz brought it to me with love. I can't give it away."

"Put it in a closet or something."

"I can't just hide it and forget about it, Bernard."

"I don't get why you feel so attached to her."

"Bernard. Listen." Her wine glass began to tip. Bernard took it from her and set it on the table. She looked down at the upholstery, tracing the pattern of leaves with a finger. "Here's how I found out that Liz was moving away." Her voice faded, and she cleared her throat. "One day she wasn't in school. I ran to her house as soon as I got off the bus and rang the doorbell. No one answered, which was not unusual, so I just went in. Her mom was sitting in the recliner in the living room, crying. She was still wearing her nightgown. I'd never seen a grown woman sob like that. I went upstairs. Liz was in her sisters' bedroom, taking all the clothes out of the dressers and laying them in suitcases. She was crying too. She told me her dad had left and was living with another woman. She said they were going down to Marietta." Revati lifted her eyes to Bernard. "I . . . didn't know how to react. I ran home, upstairs to my room, and actually crawled under the bed." She covered her face with her hands. "I stayed there until my mother called me down to dinner."

Bernard rested his hand on Revati's knee. "You were young, too."

Revati reached for the crystal vase. It was cold and heavy. She cradled it on her lap.

*

They joined the hordes of cherry-blossom viewers along the path around the Tidal Basin. After walking for about twenty minutes, Liz needed to sit down. Arsha and Bernard continued on around.

"My knees bother me when I walk a lot," Liz said. Their bench was under a small tree thickly laden with blossoms. They admired the pale pink lace of the trees around the shining pool, framing the white dome of the Jefferson Memorial. "It's like a picture postcard," Liz said. She picked up a twig with two flowers that had fallen on the bench beside her, and twirled it slowly in her fingers. Crowds streamed past in both directions. Many were East Asian—perhaps Japanese—and South Asian.

"Everyone around here seems real educated," Liz remarked. "I'm going to be like that someday. I'm looking into training for a better job."

"What kind of job are you thinking about?"

"Oh, I don't know. In computers, maybe."

"That's neat, Liz."

"Yeah." Liz coughed. "I'm afraid I won't be able to learn anything new, though."

"Why not?"

"I'm pretty sure I have a learning disability. Don't you remember how hard it was for me to spell anything?"

"I figured spelling wasn't your thing." Revati curled and uncurled the loose end of her waist pack strap.

"I'm not a smart person like you. Learning doesn't come easy for me."

"But you don't like your job, right? So, you want to go into something else."

"I like the job. The people I work with are real nice, and it's kind of fun to organize all the things we sell, the sheets and towels and little fixtures for your bathroom. When we get deliveries it's like Christmas. I love opening all the boxes. The part I don't like is having to send stuff back to the warehouse if it didn't sell. That seems sad to me."

"Overall, though, you like your job." She rolled the strap into a tight spiral.

Liz shrugged. "Sure."

"Then why do you want a different career?"

"I never thought this is all I'd be doing. I thought I'd be somebody. You know?"

"You are somebody." Revati released the strap and it unfurled. "You're the most compassionate person I've ever met. I don't know of anyone who has taken care of a dying father who abandoned them."

Liz waved her flowering twig in the air. "I don't even want to remember that. It was the most depressing thing I ever did."

"When you were a kid, what did you dream of doing?"

Liz coughed into her elbow and cleared her throat. "I had impossible dreams. I wanted to be like all the famous people I ever heard about. Florence Nightingale and Harriet Tubman. I wanted to do something that would make a big difference."

"I had no idea, Liz. You never told me."

"You were so much smarter than me. I was shy to tell you my dreams."

*

Revati carried the stepstool into the living room and climbed up, clutching Liz's vase under an arm. She managed to slide it onto the top of the bookshelf. There weren't any books up there since it was so hard to reach. When she descended and tilted her head to see the vase, she realized she'd probably never bother to get it down to use it. She didn't want to leave Liz's gift up there, forgotten, to get dustier and dustier. She stepped up again and grappled against the deeply etched hearts and doves for a finger-hold, trying to tip it onto her palm. It was heavy and slippery. She was afraid she'd cause it to fall and shatter. So, she left it there in its unreachable, almost unseeable space.

*

Throughout the week, Revati received several messages a day from Liz. Sometimes it was mundane news: "We got a shipment of towels in the strangest color" The actual color of the towels was not mentioned. Many of her messages asked unanswerable questions. One day it was: "What do you do when you have no one to love and no one loves you" Another day: "Do you believe in heaven and hell"

Revati put off replying. By Friday she still had not responded to Liz. "I guess your real busy" Liz wrote.

That evening Revati dialed Liz's number. After chatting for a few minutes, Revati got right to the point. "Liz, you sound depressed. You've been through a lot and you need help. I think it might be good for you to schedule an appointment with a counselor."

Liz huffed on the other end of the line. "It's not so bad."

*

Revati lay in bed staring at the ceiling in the darkness. "Why's she so passive?" she asked Bernard. "It seemed like she wanted my help, but now she can't even take the time to look at a few books."

"Most people don't want to make changes in their lives." He put his arm around Revati and pulled her towards him for a kiss.

She pushed away. "I feel like I'm failing her again. If I were really her best friend, I'd do whatever it took to get her out of this rut. I'd go up there and make sure she got help. I don't want to, though. I don't want to take time away from my own life to support her that much. I don't love her enough for that. So I sent her a couple of books. She doesn't even like to read."

"She's got some pretty big emotional wounds. She's got to start loving herself first." Bernard reached for her. She rolled out of his grasp, sat up and put her feet on the floor.

"Where're you going?"

She didn't answer. She didn't even know what she was so upset about. Wasn't Bernard right? She was making too big of a deal about this.

She wandered into the hallway and found herself in Arsha's bedroom. The girl had kicked the covers into a corner and lay curled on the mattress, still in her jeans and T-shirt. On the floor was a half-made poster surrounded by markers with their caps off. Revati surveyed the scene. She ought to put away the markers. She ought to try to undress Arsha.

Instead, she sank onto the bed and leaned over her daughter. She put a hand on the tangled hair and bent to kiss her cheek, closing her eyes, trying to swallow the lump in her throat. She'd never visited Liz in Marietta—had never, in fact, been to the town at all—but in her mind she pictured Liz calling that dog of hers. Liz, still a skinny sixth grader with a blonde mullet, stood with her back to the viewer and looked to the horizon, where rolling green fields met a blue, cloudless sky. There was no dog in sight. Hands cupping her mouth, she called "Revati! RAY-vuh-tee!" The name echoed silently in the air.

PERFECT SUNDAY

At the end of the day yesterday, as we were eating dinner at the only open restaurant in Elk River (an old logging town-turned-hunter's vacation paradise), my seven-year-old son, Ranjan, said, "This was the best Sunday I've ever had in my entire life."

We had decided on a whim to go see Elk Creek Falls. I came home around noon from taking the kids to Sunday school. Ranjan attended a Jewish session, and I took the three-year-old, Samir, to a little Hindu "baby chanting" class while we waited for Ranjan to be done. Who would have thought we'd find both Jewish and Hindu communities here in this little college town in northern Idaho? I tried not to think about how we might have to move away soon.

I'd brought home Ranjan's Sunday school friend, Elliot, for the afternoon. My husband, Daniel, was sweeping out the garage, so we left the car in the driveway and got out. It was a sunny, breezy day, the yard dappled with yellow aspen leaves. With the yellow leaves still on the trees, it looked like the whole place was suffused with sun. I remembered this from last year, soon after we'd moved into this house—the beautiful aspens making fall so golden. The air was fresh, too. The field-burning, which made everything smell hot and smoky, must be finished.

"I think we're going to be OK," Daniel said. He'd spent the morning paying bills. We were on the edge with our finances because Daniel's job had been downgraded to part-time, although he still spent all day at the office trying to wrestle things into shape. Since then, I had been looking for work but had yet to land a job. "I know things will be turning around with me really soon," he said, dragging the recycling boxes away from the wall and sweeping behind them. He shoved the boxes back and moved on to the kids' wheeled toys.

I stood in the driveway, reluctant to leave the sunshine and step into the dark garage. I hated being unsettled like this, not knowing what was going to happen with our finances or our lives. My dad always said, "These Americans love to take risks." I resented his stereotype. Dad acted as though he'd just come over from India recently, as though he hadn't been living in this country for almost forty years, as though he didn't finally become an American citizen himself ten years ago. Still, Dad was right in the sense that Daniel took a big risk in leaving his tenure-track job in DC to take the helm of a new regional economic development organization out here. I'd been nervous about Daniel's decision. I was more like my dad in the sense of being risk-averse. But I'd also wanted to get out of DC. Unfortunately, shortly after we'd arrived the economy tanked, much of the funding for the organization dried up, and if Daniel couldn't raise more money, he'd be out of a job entirely within months.

"Let's rake leaves!" Ranjan shouted. He and Elliot ran for the rake leaning against one wall of the garage.

"Me too!" Samir yelled. I had to separate the three of them and get them to agree to take turns. I gave Samir and Elliot brooms to use in the meantime. They all ran out on the lawn and began pushing leaves around.

"At least we're here for the time being," I said. We'd worked so hard to leave DC, to sell our overpriced little house and leave behind terrorism threats, crime, bad schools, and awful traffic. We'd made it. We had bought our house, our wonderful spacious house with three bedrooms and two and a half bathrooms and actual closets! "Maybe we'll get lucky and we won't have to move again."

"We're already lucky," he said. "Don't worry so much. Let's go somewhere today and enjoy this beautiful weather."

We decided on Elk Creek Falls. I went inside to call Elliot's mother to tell her of our plans, and to pack some lunch and snacks. Daniel got the kids buckled in and took his place behind the wheel.

The drive was beautiful, the black road unwinding like a ribbon between the yellow fields and hills. I breathed and tried to will myself to be calm. We'll be OK, we'll be OK. As we drove, the dark pine-covered hills in the distance stayed still, never seeming to come closer to us.

"We'd have to drive for hours from DC to get to anyplace like this," Daniel said.

The kids were quiet in the back, listening to Raffi on the CD player singing about six little ducks that he once knew. There were almost no other cars on the road. At one point, a bright yellow field rose up against the sky and that was all there was out that side of the window: the luminous field on the hill against the pale blue sky. I almost pointed it out to everyone. But I didn't. Let people enjoy it on their own, I thought, without my exhortations to look and to appreciate.

"I've got a new idea for fundraising," Daniel said. "With the foundations drying up like this, we've gotta get creative."

I didn't really want to think about Daniel's work. It was too depressing. But, to be supportive, I said, "That's great." Daniel launched into his idea, which involved some sort of new Internet tool.

I passed back sandwich quarters as the kids requested them. "Do you want peanut butter and jelly, or cheese and mustard?" I called.

The pine trees were black and green around us. We drove through little towns that hardly made a mark on the landscape, a few low houses and long metal buildings and then the town was gone. I was still amazed at the fact that we were in *Idaho*, of all places!

Just before we reached the town of Elk River, we saw a sign for Elk Creek Falls and turned down a gravel road into the Clearwater National Forest. "We'll have to wash the car again," Daniel said. There were so many gravel roads in Idaho. You went on an afternoon trip and came back with your car caked in dust.

We parked and got everyone out of the car. I carried the bag with water and snacks. The three boys trotted down the path through the trees. Daniel took the bag of snacks from me and grasped my hand. "How are things going with you?" he asked. "We hardly get a chance to talk."

"I've been sending out applications." I kicked a stone as we walked. I didn't want to tell him that I'd been applying for work all over the country. He was still determined to stay here.

"Any news about that marketing job at the university?" He squeezed my hand.

"If I'd had any good news, I would have told you about it already."

Daniel was silent. I didn't mean to snap at him. I'd pinned a lot of hopes on that marketing job, which would pay enough, with Daniel's part-time income, to keep us here. I had trouble being optimistic about my future, the way he usually was with his own.

"I'm just afraid," I said.

"Of what?" Now Daniel sounded exasperated.

"You know. Our finances."

"Things are going to be *fine*. I've got that big grant coming in soon. We can hold out until then."

"That grant isn't big enough for you to get paid for full-time work. And what happens when that runs out?"

"You worry too much." He tried to put an arm around my waist, but I veered out of his grasp.

"You don't worry enough," I retorted.

"Worrying isn't going to help. The universe will take care of us."

"God helps those who help themselves."

"It's a beautiful day," Daniel said. "We're in the woods. The kids are happy. We all have enough to eat."

We'd had this same conversation so many times, with no resolution. He was right that worrying wouldn't help, but his cheerfulness bugged me. How could he be so happy when it was his fault we were in this mess? He'd wanted this job, even though he knew it was risky. Yet I couldn't have the satisfaction of pinning all the blame on him. I had to admit that I'd wanted to leave, too. I'd imagined that our new life would be a kind of paradise. How had paradise turned into just the usual stress and anxiety?

"Isn't there some god you can pray to?" he asked. "Who's that Hindu god who gets rid of obstacles?"

"Ganesha," I said.

"Why don't you say a prayer to him?"

We had just learned a prayer to Ganesha during Samir's Sunday school. "Shri Vakratunda, Mahakaaya," I began. Samir looked around at the familiar words and tune. I didn't want to continue. I didn't get the sense that Ganesha cared whether or not I had obstacles in my path.

"Sing it, Mommy," Samir urged.

"Shri Vakratunda, Mahakaaya," I started again. "Koti Surya, Samaprabha." The song stuck in my throat.

"Sing it!" Samir shouted.

"You sing, if you want to."

Daniel stopped, let go of my hand, and took the camera out of his jacket pocket. Immediately all three children were flailing themselves at him.

"Me! I want to take a picture!"

"My turn! Give it to me!"

Daniel held the camera above his head. "The batteries are almost out. Daddy will take the picture. Go stand over by that big fallen tree."

The kids clambered on the log and Daniel centered them in the frame. The camera whirred.

"Let me see! Let me see!" They were flailing themselves at him again.

Daniel squatted down, camera in his palms, and they all hunched over it. I looked over Daniel's shoulder too. Cute—the three of them, with their jackets in primary colors, against the brown and green of the woods.

The older boys ran ahead. Ranjan shouted, "Cadabra!" Elliot began making shooting noises with his mouth. They were apparently playing an imaginary Pokemon game, without the cards, when they saw something on the ground and squatted. Samir raced to join them.

"A monster worm!" Elliot shouted.

When we reached the boys, they were observing the progress of a fat, fuzzy caterpillar across the forest path.

"That's a woolly bear," I said. "See how it has a red band across the middle?"

"A what? A wildebeest?" Elliot asked.

"Haven't you ever seen a woolly bear? Are they not so common anymore?" I straightened up to look at Daniel.

He shrugged. "I think they're more common back east. It'll turn into an Isabella tiger moth."

"Like Isabella in my class?" Ranjan asked. He and Elliot both started giggling.

As we walked down through the trees, we began hearing the falls crashing in the distance, very faint at first. The kids ran ahead, stopping to listen, looking around corners to find it.

At the lookout, white water fell into a black onyx pool at the bottom, set among the yellow grass, dark pine trees, and black basalt rock. The kids climbed on the railings, and I held Samir's arm as he tried to imitate the older boys. "Be careful," I shouted above the din of the waterfall. "Don't fall down the ravine."

"If he fell, he'd go rolling and bumping all the way down," Ranjan observed.

I imagined what it would have been like to have come across this waterfall without the benefit of trails or railings. Had Lewis and Clark seen this? Just a waterfall suddenly in the wilderness.

We had our snack there, sitting on a leaning bench: apple slices, crackers, and cookies.

"I brought honey." I unzipped a baggie within which was a plastic container.

"Really?" Daniel asked. "Why?"

"Rosh Hashanah is coming up." I always kept better track of Jewish holidays than Daniel did.

"We had apples and honey at Sunday school," Ranjan said.

He dragged a piece of apple through the honey in the bowl and lifted it, dripping, into his mouth. A string of stickiness fell onto his jacket.

Daniel selected an apple slice, dabbed it, and offered it to me. "We'll have a sweet year," he said. "And then I'll get to say, 'I told you so.'"

"Be my guest." I leaned over and took a bite of the apple Daniel held. The honey was smooth on my tongue.

As we walked back up, Daniel fed the kids bits of cookies every so often to keep them going. Dan thought this was very funny, that the kids could be persuaded to walk—even run— up the hill a certain distance for another crumb. There were no whole cookies left at that point.

We went to the Elk River Café for dinner, where we were the only customers. It was a little shack with old saws decorating the walls. One of them was painted with an animal scene. All three kids ordered chicken strips. Ranjan asked the server what shape of French fries would be served. "I like the straight kind," he said. "With no skin."

"I'll make sure to straighten 'em out for ya," she said, and winked at us. After putting in our order, she brought out paper cups full of crayons. Samir scribbled industriously on his paper placemat, Ranjan drew a giant woolly bear caterpillar, and Elliot worked on a portrait of his mother, with black hair, round circles of pink on her cheeks, and her lips puckered, ready to give him a kiss.

When the food arrived, Elliot made a concoction of ketchup, barbecue sauce, and ranch dressing. A white-haired man in a stained apron came out to visit with us. "Everything OK, folks?"

"Try my sauce," Elliot said.

The cook stepped agreeably to Elliot's side, picked up a French fry, dipped, bit, and looked thoughtfully up at the ceiling. "Terrific!" he proclaimed. Elliot beamed.

It was just after the cook ambled back into the kitchen that Ranjan declared the day to be the best Sunday he'd ever had. Daniel agreed. At first, I was somewhat astonished. How could this day be so wonderful when we had such a big problem looming over our heads?

Then, looking at my son's clear face, filled with calm certainty, I realized that we'd done a good job of shielding our kids from our troubles. Ranjan had no doubt that a day in the woods with a friend was about as good as it got.

On the drive home the sun was setting and since we were heading west, we had a long sunset. The sky was blue above us, turning to glowing yellow ahead as the road met the horizon. The pine trees rose past us like black lace against the fading sky. Raffi sang about snow falling on Douglas Mountain.

It had been a wonderful day, as Ranjan had said, and I thought, what if we died now, like in that movie, *The Unbearable Lightness of Being,* where they crashed their car after having a perfect evening dancing?

But we didn't die. We got back to town, dropped Elliot off, and apologized to his parents for bringing him home so late (7:45, as opposed to 7:00, which we'd promised). Then we went home and got ready for bed.

By 9:30 this morning, I was back at my desk scouring the employment sites of universities, organizations—anyone who might need marketing help. Ranjan was at school, Samir was at his morning preschool, Daniel was at his office. I got an e-mail from a place in Arkansas, asking to set up a phone interview, and I did a search of the town before replying with convenient times. Then, just after I'd hit the send button, I received an e-mail from the marketing department of the University of Idaho, telling me that while my credentials were impressive, they had chosen another candidate.

I deleted the e-mail reflexively, then un-deleted it. I wondered whether to forward this to Daniel. I decided to let him
work in peace. I closed my eyes. Ganesha, please help. I don't
know what to do. I felt like a bit of a fool, praying only when
things got difficult. Would Ganesha hold that against me?

I opened my eyes and glanced out the window. It glowed
with bright leaves. I stepped to the windowsill and, looking
down, saw that our back lawn was littered in gold.

HAWK

JULY

On the morning of a clear day at the outskirts of a Mid-western city, an elderly but still vigorous woman watched a large bird through her bedroom window. She'd awoken early and was already showered and dressed, although there was no longer anywhere she needed to be. The bird glided on a drift of air over the path by the creek, the distinct scallops of the dark wings and tail outlined against the sky.

The woman wore black stretch pants and a polo shirt which displayed, above her left breast, the logo of the Lincoln County Medical Center. Her hair was a short gray cap. Her tan skin didn't look wrinkled so much as carved. On her wrist was a watch with a round white dial and red second hand. She wore no jewelry. She stood with her feet apart, hands on hips, as though ready to order someone into action.

Once the bird floated out of sight, she turned to face the room, strewn with cardboard boxes, some sealed shut and some open and empty. She scratched her head and bent over a planner open on the nightstand. At the 1:00 mark, one word: Manisha. She straightened, nodded once, and cast her eyes at a framed photo on her dresser, a laughing baby in a frilly dress. She closed her eyes. Two fine lines appeared on her forehead.

*

Shortly after one o'clock, Manisha pulled her minivan into the driveway of the tan house she'd grown up in, one of many on this curving street with a jutting two-car garage as its most prominent feature. She slid closed the door of her vehicle and surveyed the scene. She was thin and athletic, with long black hair and skin a few shades darker than her mother's. She wore cropped jeans and a crisp tailored blouse. Diamonds glinted on her earlobes, and a gold and diamond tennis bracelet graced one wrist.

The yard had no flowers. Only mature, prickly juniper bushes pressed against the house. A metal sign had been stabbed into the front lawn: For Sale. And splashed diagonally across: SOLD.

She let herself into the house and kicked off her sandals in the entryway. The air smelled of toasted spices: cumin, mustard seeds, turmeric, curry leaves. Sealed cardboard boxes were stacked on the tile floor. Beyond them, the beige living room carpet revealed dents in several places. Furniture had recently been removed.

Upstairs, her mother sat on a neatly made bed, sorting through items in a drawer which had been pulled out of the dresser.

"Hi." Manisha put her purse on the dresser next to her

baby photo. "Sorry I'm late. Charlotte was being clingy when I dropped her off at camp."

The older woman lifted a pile of receipts and papers from the drawer.

"I'll work on the closet." Manisha made her way through the crowd of cardboard boxes.

Her mother extracted a tiny plastic case from the drawer. Holding it aloft, she said, "What I don't understand is: why sixth grade? You have earned a PhD. You have published papers. Why middle school?" Her accent was Indian, with hard consonants and rolled Rs. Her pronunciation was careful and precise.

Manisha set a hand on her hip. "Don't start again."

"You have not given me a good explanation."

She blew air out her lips and tossed back her hair. "I like to teach."

"And this place does not even have a high school. You will not be able to move to higher grades."

"I enjoy working with children."

"You don't feel you will be wasting your education?" Her mother opened the little plastic case.

Manisha coaxed a stack of sweaters down from the closet shelf and into her arms. "I'm tired of being an adjunct. I need benefits since Gerard and I separated."

"You are still married. He should provide you with benefits."

"I don't want to depend on him anymore." Manisha dropped the sweaters into an empty box.

Her mother picked out the shiny item from the foam of the case in her hand. "Why spend so many years getting a PhD in English literature if you wanted to teach children?" She held out, on the palm of her hand, a square golden object. "Here is your Phi Beta Kappa key. Don't you want it?"

Manisha kneeled to press the sweaters into the box. "Mom. This is why I don't try to explain my life to you. I got the PhD because, if you recall, you wanted a Dr. in front of my name one way or another." She stood and approached the closet.

The room filled with the soft sounds of papers scraping against the wood of the drawer, and empty hangers clicking. Manisha dumped a pile of clothes on the bed and began folding them.

Her mother pulled an envelope from the drawer and tilted it back and forth to look at both sides. "I was going to give you this at your high school graduation." She held it up for Manisha to see. "But . . . I did not think you would want it then. We were having so many conflicts. If you don't want it now, I will recycle it." She tossed it across the bed to her daughter. It landed on top of a folded blouse.

The business envelope had browned with age. Manisha stared at it for a moment. She glanced at her mother, busy with the drawer again. She picked up the envelope and felt the soft, old paper. Tucking a lock of hair behind her ear, she sank to the bed. As she worked her thumb under the glued-down flap, the weakened paper of the envelope ripped in two.

Her eyes shifted to her mother again. The older woman seemed not to have heard the sound of paper tearing.

Manisha eased the folded letter out of the jagged gap and flattened it on the bedspread. It had been written on hospital letterhead. The date in the upper right corner caught her eye. "You wrote this when I was one year old?"

Her mother had lifted from the drawer a little velvet bag.

Manisha tapped the date. "I thought you said you were going to give it to me when I graduated from—"

"Just after your father died, I wanted to put into words what we both wished for you." She pressed the velvet bag to her lap. "I thought it would be a nice thing for you when you became an adult. Something to keep in mind."

Propped against one wall near the closet was an unfinished oil portrait of a dark brown man, with a small black and white snapshot of the same man taped to a corner of the canvas. Manisha's eyes traveled to the painting. She shook her head. "I wish I could've finished that. The expression on his face . . . I kept painting over it, and . . ."

"You don't remember what he looked like. And we don't have many pictures of him. He was always the one behind the camera."

Manisha closed her eyes, and then shifted her glance to the letter. She scanned the faded cursive ink. "I want you to do even better than we have done," her mother had written. "You must stand on our shoulders and reach higher. You do not have to be bound by tradition. You can do anything you choose. The whole world is open to you. Thomas Jefferson said, 'Nothing can stop the man with the right mental attitude from achieving his goal; nothing on earth can help the man with the wrong mental attitude.' You will have the right mental attitude. You were born in the land of freedom. No outdated traditions will stand in your way." The letter repeated similar vague phrases over and over again.

The letter was signed, "Bhagya Venkataraman, MD" and below this, in parentheses, "(your loving mother)." Manisha frowned and touched the signature. "You saw yourself as a doctor first, and a mother second."

Bhagya froze for a moment. Her eyes blazed. Then she set down the velvet bag, stepped around the corner of the bed, and lifted the letter from the bedspread. "Maybe things would have been different if he had lived." She folded it and angled it into the torn envelope. "That first year at home with you was so difficult for me. You were very fussy." She resumed her seat. "He would come home, pick you up, walk around with you, hum softly, and then you would sleep."

Manisha's left thumb reached for the palm side of her ring finger to adjust her wedding ring. It was not there. She opened her hand on her knee and gazed at the lines: life, heart, head.

"What a relief for me to go back to work. Maybe if he had lived, I could have taken more time with you and learned to be a better mother." Bhagya went to set the letter in the drawer, but did not release it from her grasp. "I did my best. Even though I hired nannies to look after you, I always made time to cook Indian food. I was not going to raise you on bread and noodles and packaged meals." Bhagya thrust the envelope at Manisha. "Take it if you wish. Otherwise I will throw it away."

Manisha's hands remained on her knees as she frowned at the envelope. She reached over the drawer for it as her mother pulled it back, and they both tugged at it for a second. The letter in its envelope ripped in two. Manisha grabbed both pieces and fit them together on the bedspread in front of her, pressing her palm over the jagged tear. "Mom." She cleared her throat. "I know you worked hard to send me to a prep school. Even though I didn't feel like I fit in, I do appreciate what you did for me."

Bhagya straightened her spine. "What do you mean, you didn't fit in? Your grades were very good."

"It was essentially a school for privileged white boys. The rest of us were on the fringes."

"You were allowed to participate in everything." Bhagya fingered the velvet bag again.

"You think they'd ever cast a brown girl as the lead in the school musical?"

"I did not want you to waste your time fooling around with drama." Bhagya loosened the drawstring of the bag.

Manisha traced the ragged edge of one half of the letter. "That's why I'm so excited to be teaching at this school, Mom.

Newton is modern. I can be a role model here, not only to minority students, but to everyone."

Bhagya shook something from the bag onto her palm. She held up what looked to be a large coin. "This is the gold medal I won."

Manisha peered at it. "I've never seen that before."

"Take it in your hand," Bhagya offered.

She accepted the medal, about the size of a silver dollar, and weighed it on her palm. "It's heavy."

"Gold is heavier than other metals."

Manisha brushed her thumb over the etched letters spelling out Mysore Medical College, and over the caduceus, two winged serpents twined around a staff. "Wow. So, this was an award for—"

"Surgery. I was best in my class."

"You never told me this, Mom." Manisha held up the coin so that it appeared in the air beside her mother's face.

"On the day I won this, I brought it home to show my family, and my mother offered to have it melted to make a pair of earrings. Can you imagine! My mother did not see the value of a medal. 'What is the use of keeping this gold in a box?' she said. 'A woman should wear jewelry.'" Bhagya touched her bare earlobe. "I never cared for all that. After my marriage, and before I came to the US, I distributed all my jewelry to my sisters." She held out her hand for the medal. "You are more like my mother, in a way. You wanted a diamond bracelet for your college graduation."

From downstairs, a clock chimed the half-hour. Manisha, frowning, returned the medal to her mother. Her diamond bracelet winked as it slid down her arm. Bhagya dropped the coin in the bag and tugged the drawstring tight.

"So, Mom." Manisha stood and stuffed the letter into her back pocket. "What're you planning to do with yourself once you move to your new place? Since you retired you've kept busy selling the house and buying the condo."

"I didn't retire," she said.

"OK. Since you left your job."

"I was pushed out. The medical director questioned my judgment, and asked me to leave."

"Do you want to tell me what that was all about?"

"I'm not ready to say anything yet." Bhagya kneeled on the carpet in front of the dresser. She tugged open a drawer, revealing shimmering colors: her silk saris. "I will never wear these again. Give them to Goodwill."

Manisha shook her head. "Goodwill doesn't want your saris. You should keep them. Maybe now you'll have time to attend some of those Indian events—"

"I don't fit in with other Indians." Fingertips on top of the dresser, she pulled herself to a stand, grunting at the effort. "For them, it is all about gods and temples. You know how I feel about that."

Manisha crossed her arms over her chest. "What'll you do once you're settled in the condo?"

"I plan to write the story of my life."

Manisha laughed. "What life? All you ever did was work."

Bhagya fixed her with an icy glare.

Manisha dropped her gaze and faced the empty closet.

"The story of my work life, then." Bhagya sat on the bed again, upended the drawer and dumped out its contents. "I have things to say that other people may be interested in. Even if you are not."

"It'll keep you busy, I guess. So that's good." Manisha bit her lip. Then, turning to face her mother, she opened her mouth, as though to say something. But the room remained silent.

AUGUST

Manisha stood in a sleek dining hall, bright with sunlight streaming through the floor-to-ceiling windows. Around her in the room on this Sunday afternoon milled parents, kids, teachers, and administrators. The hum of conversation hung in the air. A group of girls sprawled on the floor in a corner, eating cookies and giggling. It was the Back to School Social.

"So, you're Wilson's new language arts teacher." A gray-haired man clapped his large white hand on the shoulder of a boy in shorts and sandals. The man's small eyes darted from Manisha's face, to her yellow tunic, white pants, and flats.

"We're so pleased to meet you." Wilson's mother held out a manicured hand. "I'm Abby Lewis, and this is my father, John Wilson." The woman's shoulder-length hair glistened as though someone had brushed it with liquid gold. She wore high-heeled sandals, a sleeveless blouse, and a knee-length skirt.

Manisha held out her hand to Wilson. "I'm Ms. V. It's nice to meet you. I guess you're named after your grandfather."

The boy, smiling shyly, glanced up at his mother, and then put his thin white hand into Manisha's. "I liked the summer reading book," he said softly to her elbow.

"*The Giver*? I'm glad."

"I've never seen him so excited about an assigned book," Abby said.

Wilson looked up at his mother again. "Can I go outside?"

"Shoo." She laughed and patted him on the back. He darted out the door to the playground on the other side of the windows. While the elementary kids monopolized the slides and monkey bars, the middle schoolers dribbled basketballs or bounced four-square balls. Brown and tan legs flashed occasionally among the white and pink limbs.

John Wilson squinted at Manisha. "I try to keep up with

the new hires, but . . . where did you teach previously?"

"I was at the university for many years," she replied.

"And . . . where are you from, originally?"

Abby smiled. "My dad's one of the founders of this school, so he—"

"Abby." He tapped her shoulder with his fist.

"I'm sorry." Abby looked into the distance, tracing an eyebrow with one finger.

Manisha smiled. "I understand what you're asking. I was born and raised right here in this city."

The grandfather tilted back and forth on his white tennis shoes and seemed about to say something else. Abby shifted her gaze over her father's shoulder and waved to someone. "Dad, remember, you wanted to introduce me to—"

John Wilson stepped away from both his daughter and Manisha. "I'm going to get something to eat."

Abby and her father walked away in different directions, and their places were taken by a couple in androgynous clothes: both wore knee-length shorts, untucked button-down shirts, and hiking sandals. Both had light brown hair streaked with gray. With them was their daughter, a tan Asian girl with black bobbed hair and a pair of rectangular black glasses.

Manisha bent her knees, peered at the girl, and laughed. "Kay, I just discovered something. Your glasses have no lenses."

Kay grinned and shrugged her shoulders.

"She wants to be like Harriet the Spy," the mother said, ruffling her daughter's hair.

Kay nodded happily up at her mother.

"I love Harriet the Spy too," Manisha said.

"I've read it five times!" Kay hopped on one foot.

"I'm looking forward to being your teacher." Manisha held out her right hand. Kay grasped the fingertips for a second, and then dashed away to join the girls sprawled on the floor in the corner.

After a few more pleasantries, Kay's parents wandered away, and Manisha strolled to the food table where Donna, a short, white-haired woman, stood holding a plastic cup of punch.

"How's it going so far?" Donna asked.

"Fine, I think. I just met Kay's parents."

"They are so sweet." She sipped. "I must admit, I'm not quite ready to be back. I had such a glorious summer." She swirled the liquid in her cup. "What I really need right now is a glass of wine." She leaned closer and whispered, "See that couple over there?"

Manisha noticed an overweight woman and man, both in baggy shorts, talking to Pauline, the head of the school. The woman wore a flowered blouse, and the man was in a polo shirt which draped over his belly.

"Huge funders," Donna murmured. "Their kids don't do much work, though. They fail every quarter, and somehow the grades get adjusted. Their daughter Izzie is over there." Donna pointed to the girls in the corner. "She's the one with the blonde curls. Those are all sixth graders. Your students." The girls wore tight knee-length jeans shorts or calf-length leggings, and knit tops embellished with sequins or ruffles. Their empty plates and cups had been tossed outside their circle, a moat of trash to protect them from the rest of the crowd. Kay, her back supported against the wall, sat with a small reporter's notebook pressed against her upraised knees.

"Kay seems to be taking notes," Manisha said.

Donna laughed. "We've got several quirky students, and for the most part they're accepted. Watch out for Aliya and Emma. They're best friends, but also competitors for alpha female. Emma, especially, will try to push other girls around if she gets a chance."

Aliya, with bright brown eyes and dark hair, waved her plump hands as she spoke. Emma rolled her eyes and stretched her legs into the middle of the circle so her sandals almost grazed Aliya's knee.

Outside the moat of trash, a dark brown girl with a long, glossy black braid stood observing the circle of friends. She wore a pair of boys' knit shorts and an oversized orange T-shirt with a narwhal imprinted on it.

"Who's that?" Manisha asked.

"She's new this year. Her name is Nirali, I believe. She seems a little awkward. I'd keep an eye on her, at least until she settles in."

Nirali caught Kay's eye and gave a small wave. Kay wrinkled her nose and scowled at the notebook balanced on her upraised knee.

*

In the almost-empty living room of her new condo, sitting cross-legged on the sofa, Bhagya wrote on a yellow legal pad with a felt-tip pen. Next to her on the cushion sat a battered dictionary, its hardbound spine coming loose. The walls around her were blank and white. On the polished wood floor stood one end table with a lamp. No rug. No other furniture. The curtains of the sliding glass door were open, and outside, a bare concrete-floored patio with high privacy walls.

The pendulum of the clock on the mantle ticked back and forth. The pen scratched softly against the paper.

I have spent over 35 years as an OB-GYN. I am 75. My health is good. I could have continued working. But they questioned my judgment. The medical director says that I am in the beginning stages of

She crossed out this last sentence, picked up the dictionary, and consulted it for some minutes. Then she began again on the next line.

He did not actually say "dementia," but he mentioned my memory. There is nothing wrong with my memory. He also said my hands were not steady enough for surgery. There is nothing wrong with my hands.

She held up her long, sinewy fingers against the light from the sliding door. She flexed them, stretched them, and took up her pen again.

I was a pioneer at that hospital. Under my leadership, birth outcomes were excellent. And I am still a pioneer. My story will prove that.

Ever since I was a little girl, my ambition was to be a physician. There was a lady doctor who took care of my mother quite often. Amma tended to miscarry, so this woman became almost part of our family. She would come to the house. I admired her. She was gentle and confident. I thought my mother gave in too much to my father and his mother. I wanted Amma to stand up for herself. As the oldest child, I had to be strong to protect my mother. And this lady doctor . . . sometimes I imagined she was my mother.

In India at that time, there weren't many career choices for girls. Medicine was considered a good field for women, because it involved nurturing. In our family, nursing was not an option. It was considered menial. The pay was too low. And the other option was to study home science or get some kind of bachelor's degree just to say you have a degree, and then get married and stay home raising the children. I was

*not interested in that. My father wanted me to be highly edu-
cated. I was the eldest of three daughters. I was to set a good
example for my sisters. My uncles did not agree that I should
become a doctor, but I did not care what they thought. I had
my father's support. As it happened, I was the only one who
pursued a career. My sisters got married immediately after
college and never earned money.*

The dryer buzzed from the laundry nook off the kitchen.
She glared in that direction until it stopped, and then turned
back to her notepad.

*I was one of twenty women students in a class of almost
100 at the medical college, and all the women students
assumed we would go into obstetrics. Sometimes people in the
US are surprised that there are so many women doctors from
India. They do not realize that almost all the obstetricians in
India are women. An Indian woman does not want to expose
herself to a man.*

*When I finished medical school, I applied to residency
programs in Bangalore. I was not accepted. There were not
enough slots in these programs. Some of my classmates applied to hospitals in the United States. It was easier here to get
a slot. So, I also applied. I had the ambition to advance in my
career, and I also wanted to help my parents. My mother was
ill, my father would soon retire, and my sisters still had to be
educated and married.*

*My parents were afraid to send me abroad as a single
woman. They got me married. Venku was my classmate. It
wasn't really an arranged marriage. At least I knew him.*

Here, she stopped and looked at the pictures on the table
next to her: a framed 8 x 10 of Manisha as a teen, with long,

straight black hair, wearing a flouncy prom dress and high heels; and a black and white snapshot propped against the first, its edges browned with age, showing Venku as a young man with the Statue of Liberty in the background.

Bhagya unclenched her hands and rubbed her palms on her sweatpants. To her right, outside the glass sliding doors, a bright red bird alighted on the privacy wall surrounding the bare little patio. It had a black beak, and its head was embellished with a red crest. It tilted its tail up and down a few times, and then fluttered away. She continued to consider the empty sky.

SEPTEMBER

"You have a knack for teaching." Pauline, a stocky white woman, sat behind her desk which displayed a laptop, a basket of tiny apples, a pair of reading glasses, and a brushed metal pen holder. A brass name plaque read "Pauline Cox, Head of School."

"Thank you." Manisha, clutching a notebook and pen, smiled up at Pauline's face across the desk. She sat deep in a padded armchair which put her at a lower level than the administrator. The sunshine streaming through the window behind Pauline's desk shone in Manisha's eyes, causing her to shift her gaze away from her boss's face to focus on the sleeve of Pauline's cardigan.

Pauline lifted the reading glasses to her nose and used her mouse to scroll through a document. "The lesson was well-paced, and the kids seemed interested. You have excellent rapport with the students, and good control of the classroom. You're off to a fine start."

"Thank you," Manisha repeated.

Pauline's eyes blazed at Manisha over the top of her glasses.

The closed office door filtered the sounds of Pauline's assistant clicking her computer keys in the alcove, and beyond that, noises from a few straggling students: locker doors banging shut, shouted goodbyes.

"There are many private schools in our area, as I'm sure you know." Pauline lifted her glasses from her face, holding them aloft in the air. "We want to set ourselves apart from the others. The thing to keep in mind is, what can Newton offer to students and families that they can't get at one of the other schools?"

Manisha nodded and jotted Pauline's words into her notebook.

"As you know, our push this year is diversity. We have students from many ethnicities and cultures at this school. We want our curriculum to reflect that. I've looked at your syllabus, and while it seems solid, I'm not seeing as much diversity in terms of the literature as I'd like."

"I thought I should follow Donna's lead in my first year, since she's been here so long, and she taught sixth grade last year. She gave me the syllabus she used."

Pauline tapped the end of her earpiece against her jawbone. "We hired you because we saw something special in *you*." She smiled, eyes crinkling pleasantly. "I'd like to see *your* stamp on the curriculum. Think about it this way: what can you bring to this school that no other teacher can bring?" Pauline stood, resting her manicured fingertips on the edge of her shiny desk.

Manisha used the heels of her hands to push herself up from the padded chair. "I've got some ideas. I'll put together a new syllabus and get that to you by tomorrow morning."

"You don't need to show me anything new." Pauline escorted Manisha to the door. "We trust our teachers to do what's best. Just keep in mind what I said."

*

Standing on a stepstool on her mother's bare patio, Manisha reached up to hang the red and yellow hummingbird feeder from a hook on the privacy wall. Bhagya squatted on the concrete, filling a tube-shaped feeder with seed. Manisha carried the stool to the opposite wall, where another hook waited.

Bhagya gathered some seeds into her palm and used a forefinger to sort through them. "What is it we are feeding them?"

"Sunflower seeds, thistle, and I don't know what else. The guy at the store said it would attract cardinals, goldfinches, and other songbirds. You're going to enjoy this."

Bhagya stood, brushed her hands together, and handed the seed feeder up to Manisha. "I never had time to watch birds before."

"You need some furniture out here." Manisha stepped down and folded the stool closed. "A couple of lounge chairs, a table—"

"No." Bhagya picked up the half-empty bag of seed and slid open the glass door. "I do not want anything." Before she stepped inside, she glanced over her shoulder. Manisha's gaze tracked her mother's. A big bird was suspended in the air, sailing on still wings outlined in black against the blue sky.

"What is that called?" Bhagya asked.

"I think it's a hawk."

"I never used to look at the sky before." Bhagya shaded her eyes against the sunlight. "I never looked up. And they were there all along." She put a fist to her chest. "I feel it right here."

Manisha breathed in sharply. "It's majestic."

"Yes. That is a good word." Bhagya lifted her bare foot to step inside and stubbed her toe.

"Careful!" Manisha, carrying the stepstool, followed her mother into the living room. "Are you OK, Mom?"

Bhagya limped to the sofa and sat rubbing her toe. "I am fine."

Manisha surveyed the room. "In here, though, you definitely need something more. All you have is one old sofa and a table."

"Why do I need furniture now? We have just spent time getting rid of so much from the house."

"What happened to your beautiful teak dining table?"

"I gave it away."

"This is our old set from the basement, right?" Manisha grasped the back of a painted chair. "And where's the TV? Where are your bookshelves? I know the movers brought all those things here. I showed them where to arrange everything."

"I called that refugee resettlement organization and asked them to take those things away." Bhagya set the bag of seed on the dining table and crossed her arms over her chest.

Manisha scanned the almost empty walls of the house. No pictures had been hung up. The clock above the fireplace clicked its pendulum back and forth. "It's so bare in here that it echoes."

"I want nothing else around me."

A high-pitched ring startled both of them. "The phone," Bhagya mumbled, and walked towards the sound, into the kitchen.

As Manisha wandered into the bedroom, her mother said into the phone, "How can that be? I am sure I did not—"

The bedroom was as stark as the living room. An old twin bed and a small table. No dresser. No mirror. The chest of drawers had been placed inside the walk-in closet, in which hung a small collection of clothing.

Manisha peeked into the bathroom. A single frayed towel hung from the rod. She stepped into the living room again.

"Everything OK?" Manisha asked as her mother re-entered

the room.

"That was my bank. They say I have bounced two checks. I know it cannot be true. I am very careful with money. I will go talk to them and they will straighten it out." Bhagya settled herself on the sofa. Her short hair poufed out on one side, as though she'd been scratching her head.

"I'll make tea." In the kitchen, Manisha opened a cabinet and took down two ceramic mugs. "Where do you keep your spice box?" She looked at her mother over the breakfast bar that separated the kitchen from the living-dining area.

Bhagya frowned and rubbed her forehead with strong fingers. "I think . . . in the old house, it used to be . . ."

"Never mind. I found it." From the cabinet beside the stove, Manisha pulled out a round stainless steel container and pried off the lid. Inside were small steel bowls, each containing a separate spice. She filled the teakettle with water, added two tea bags, a few cloves, cardamom, and cinnamon pieces, and set it on the stove to boil.

Once the tea was strained, Manisha added a splash of milk to each mug and both women sat at the old dining table.

"Sugar is here." Bhagya pushed the ceramic bowl towards Manisha, who added a teaspoonful. Bhagya's hand shook when she lifted the spoon from the bowl, scattering white crystals across the table.

"How are you doing financially?" Bhagya set the spoon back into the bowl.

"We're fine. He's helping with the kids."

"Is there any hope of reconciliation? It cannot be good for the children—"

"I'm not asking for your advice, Mom."

"Why is it that you separated? You have never told me."

Manisha adjusted her mug on the coaster, so an even circle of cork appeared around the bottom rim. "I don't want to talk about it."

"Do you plan to divorce? It might be better to have a written child support agreement."

"Mom." She stood up. "I'm not an idiot. The divorce is in the works. He had an affair. He's moved in with her. There's no hope of reconciliation."

"These American men are all alike. They have no sense of commitment to—"

"I said I don't want to talk about it." She moved past her mother, into the kitchen, and began opening and closing cupboards for something to do. With her back turned to her mother, she brushed at her eyes.

"Let me know if you need any help," her mother said. "My money is yours."

"Keep your savings for yourself, Mom." Her voice quavered. She grabbed a glass from a cabinet, filled it halfway from the dispenser on the fridge door, and gulped a mouthful. Through the bottom of the glass her mother's bare new kitchen swam around her. She swallowed another sip, took a deep breath, and returned to the table.

Bhagya used the side of her hand to sweep the scattering of sugar crystals into a neat mound on the table. "Why do I need savings now?"

Manisha positioned her water glass next to her tea mug. "Let's change the subject." She looked brightly at her mother. "What is it that you'd like to do with your life now? Do you want to travel? Do you want to take classes?"

Bhagya peered into her mug and shook her head. "I am fine."

"You like to cook. Right? Sometimes you used to have little dinner parties. You'd invite people from work. I remember that."

Bhagya placed a sugar crystal on the tip of her tongue.

"Do you want to invite a few people over? The kids and I could come too. I could bring something."

"Nat and Charlotte used to like my mutter paneer," she said. "Remember how Nat wanted lemon rice whenever he came over? But now, they are growing up. They want pizza."

Manisha tapped her fingernails against the side of her mug. "How's your writing going? Have you started that yet?"

"I have begun." With a forefinger Bhagya molded the tiny mound of sugar crystals into a little line.

"Are you writing this for me?"

"It is for anyone who wants to read it. So they will know how and why we came to be here in this country."

"Who's 'they'"

"The Americans."

"We *are* Americans, Mom."

With her thumbnail, Bhagya cut tiny grooves into the line of sugar. "Yes. We are. And we are not."

*

"Donna, I'm wondering if you'd mind taking a look at this." Manisha stood on the other side of Donna's desk holding a few stapled pages with both hands, like a platter of offerings. Donna was almost shielded from view behind her computer. Two fifth-grade girls lingered in the room, using glue sticks, markers, and construction paper to create a folded object.

"What's up?" Donna asked without lifting her eyes from the screen. "Girls, you'll have to finish up and go to the library."

Manisha watched as the girls hurried to glue down one flap. They threw their supplies in a plastic bin. One of them carried the bin to the cabinet, and the other stepped behind Donna's desk to present their creation. While Donna admired it, the girl put her arm around the teacher's shoulders and rested her cheek on Donna's white curls.

"Go on, now." Donna stood up, walked the girls and their craftwork to the door, and gave each a quick hug.

"They're so attached to you!" Manisha smiled.

Donna resumed her place behind the computer and, with her hands on her lap, looked at Manisha.

"Pauline asked me to re-do my syllabus." Manisha held up the pages in her hand. "I'd like someone to look it over. I could ask her, but I get the feeling that she's not really interested in being that hands-on with the teachers."

"Let me just finish this e-mail." Donna's keyboard click-clacked as she typed. Manisha shifted her gaze from Donna's face to the window, through which she could see blue sky between the slats of the open blinds.

Donna scanned her screen, clicked one final time, stood up and extended her hand for the papers. "Pauline's most interested in golf." She ran her eyes over the print. "Her goal is to push as much work as possible to the teachers. Have you noticed that on nice days, she doesn't come in at all?"

"I didn't quite realize . . . she's not here today."

Donna flipped the page. From the hallway came the rumbling sound of a wheeled janitor's cart. The noise grew louder, and then stopped at the doorway. A young black woman dragged a vacuum cleaner into the room, the orange cord coiled around her forearm. She plugged in the machine and it roared to life.

Donna handed the pages back to Manisha. "Looks fine," she shouted.

"You think so?"

"She says she wants diversity." Donna flicked the back of her hand at the papers. "You're giving her diversity. She should be happy." She lifted a leather shoulder bag from under her desk and set it on her chair.

"Right." Manisha creased the pages lengthwise. "Of course."

*

One lamp on the end table illuminated the corner of the sofa where Bhagya sat with her yellow legal pad, but the rest of the apartment lay in darkness. The curtains over the sliding door were closed against the night outside, and the clock above the fireplace ticked its pendulum back and forth.

Dear Manisha,

You asked if I am writing this for you, and I realized that the answer is yes. I am writing this for you. It is the story of how you came to be born and raised in this country.

I should tell you that I never wanted to marry. Perhaps I should have come to this country on my own. But I was a coward. I did not want to upset my mother. So, I agreed to the wedding. Venku told me that he used to admire me in medical school. He was never among the boys who teased the girls. I did not dislike him. Once we moved to this country, I learned to cook his favorite dishes. He did all the cleaning, and in this way we managed. He was a good husband. So when he wanted a child, I agreed. It seemed only fair.

But was it fair to you? Only you can answer that question. Manisha, I have not told you much about the start of my career. Where was the time to talk? So often, by the time I came home from work, you were asleep. So, here is my story.

In India we always had the impression that America was much more advanced. I was surprised when I came to the US to encounter backward attitudes. So many people thought women didn't have the brains for medicine, and especially not for a surgical specialty. Once we were here, everyone thought I should switch to something like dermatology or pathology or radiology. Something with a fixed schedule, and without night calls. Even the other medical residents advised me against obstetrics.

One resident told me, "Women obstetricians look like men." Ridiculous.

Since I had done well in surgery, I went ahead. Venku encouraged me, and I would not be stopped by what other people said. I am still the same way. I see what needs to be done, and I do it, even if others disagree.

I went to my first residency interview wearing a new printed silk sari. I had only been in this country for a few months, and that was what I wore all the time: cotton saris at home, and polyester for going out to the store. I thought silk would be right for an interview. But after our meeting, the program director said he would

Her forehead wrinkled. She kept the pen poised over the page for several seconds. Then she exhaled, threw down the pen, opened the dictionary, and ruffled the thin pages until she came to the word she wanted. She picked up her pen and began again.

He wanted to postpone my meeting with the residency director. He said he wanted me to come back wearing Western clothes. I had to go and buy a skirt. I had to learn to shave my legs, and wear stockings.

Manisha, I want you to know that we came to this country because the Americans asked us to come. We did not invade this country. The United States had programs to train foreign medical graduates, because of the shortage of doctors in America. We are the best from our countries. There is an

American test we take. Everyone around the world takes the test on the same day every year. It is called the ECFMG. It is given by the Educational Commission for Foreign Medical Graduates. And only once you pass this test can you come to the US and receive training here.

At that time the American medical graduates got first choice of internships and residencies. The foreign graduates got what was left. We were placed in towns and hospitals which were not prestigious enough for the Americans. When medical students came to tour the hospital, they never asked any of us foreign medical graduates to lead the tours. They didn't want the students to see how many foreign doctors were at the hospital. And it was hard for us to be chosen for leadership positions, chief resident, or department chief. At that time, we did not complain. We felt we were lucky to be getting this advanced training.

Some people thought we should not be here at all. Not just the uneducated people who were afraid of those with brown skin. Even some doctors felt this way. There was one article in a medical magazine. It said that foreign doctors should go back to their own countries. But the US did not bring us here to help us serve our countries. We were taught how to treat patients in the American way, with all the equipment available here. So how could they expect me to go back to India and serve the poor? We were not trained for that. Even with the foreign doctors, still so many slots went unfilled. They needed us here. They asked us to come here. They trained us in the American way. And they said it was our fault when we stayed.

Bhagya set aside the pad of paper and propped her elbow on the arm of the sofa, snapping and unsnapping the pen cap with her thumb. Snap. Snap. Snap. The cap fell into the space between the sofa and end table. She squinted down at it. She could see the clip glinting faintly. She set the pen on the table and clutched her empty hands in her lap.

OCTOBER

Manisha was dreaming. She walked through a large building, several floors high, with glass walls and ceilings. She could see the building through the walls from the outside, as though she were floating in the sky: an Escher-like maze of white stairs, escalators, conference rooms, and hallways. At the same time, she could also see it from the inside: she rose up a white escalator, fingers clutching the railing. A few of her students descended another escalator. She waved at them. They did not notice.

She was supposed to be leading a group of students through the airport. They had tickets to go somewhere—she wasn't sure where. She had lost the students. Now, heart racing, she searched for them through those white, bright hallways, up and down stairs. She'd see glimpses of them, a blue shoe or a blonde ponytail, but when she hurried to catch up, they had disappeared again into the maze.

She opened her eyes. The room was dim. Classical music wafted from her phone alarm. She sprawled in the middle of the king bed, clutching her pillow, and placed a palm over her heart. It hammered as if she were still running through the dream airport. She moved her limbs under the covers. "You can do it," she whispered to herself. Sitting in bed, she picked up her phone and touched the alarm off.

Before showering, she ducked into each child's room. Nat had kicked off his covers. His face was buried in his pillow, and his feet stretched off the end of the bed. The room smelled like dirty clothes. Manisha made her way through the clothes on the floor to the desk, stacked a mug on a plate, and picked up a handful of energy bar wrappers.

Holding the dishes, she stepped into Charlotte's room. The little girl huddled under the covers next to an array of stuffed animals. Her thin arm clutched a large panda. The room smelled of wood shavings from the cage in the corner, and a faint whirr emanated from the hamster's exercise wheel.

Manisha pushed aside the curtains of the window and looked out on the oak tree's scarlet leaves against the cloudy sky.

*

"Did you ever wonder why parents send their kids to Newton?"

Manisha perched on a bar stool next to Donna. "I assume it's because . . . we're different from other schools," she said.

A plate of happy hour snacks sat on the counter between them. Manisha ran her fingers up and down the stem of a glass of red wine. Conversations murmured around them. Rain lashed the branches outside the windows.

Donna propped an elbow on the bar. "That's what the admissions office tells people. What's really innovative about us? We have a fancy building. We have nice furniture in the classrooms. Other than that, we're no better than a good neighborhood public school. Except that our students are a lot richer."

Manisha laughed. "Donna, I think you're a little drunk."

"Has Pauline told you yet that you were hired because you brought something special to this school?"

Manisha pulled down the corners of her mouth. "I guess she says that to everyone?"

"First-year teachers are Guinea pigs." Donna rolled a breaded mushroom off the plate and nibbled at it. "Every year the administration comes up with some new thing we're supposed to focus on. Last year it was revising our unit plans for 'understanding' and 'big questions.' Next year? Who knows?"

"And this year it's diversity?"

"The teachers who get contracts year after year are the folks who ignore the new initiatives."

Manisha smiled, and then frowned.

"Look at me. I've been at this school forever. I teach the same way today that I taught twenty-five years ago."

"I know that's not true, Donna. You've given me materials you created last year for sixth grade."

"I'm constantly revising what I do, but my fundamental teaching philosophy is the same. Get the kids excited about reading and writing. Have them do a lot of it. That's all. I'm not going to be anyone's Guinea pig."

Manisha glanced around the room, at the gas fireplace waving its flames, at the other diners hunched over their plates. She set her glass down, boosted herself off the stool and hung her purse over her shoulder. "Donna, I need to leave." She pulled her phone out of her purse and frowned at it. "I just realized that . . . I need to pick up my daughter from . . . are you going to be OK? Do you need me to drive you anywhere?"

Donna held up her empty glass and nodded at the bartender. "Frank's on his way. You go ahead."

*

Bhagya watched a small yellow bird perched on the feeder on the patio, pulling seed from the tube. The creature had a black cap and its wings, lapped over its back like a shawl, were black with thin white stripes. Several larger mottled brown birds flew up, and the yellow one darted away.

Bhagya took up her pen.

Dear Manisha,

I want you to know about the pioneering work I did during my career. I wanted to fit in, yes. I developed the attitude, "When in Rome, do as the Romans do." I never wore Indian clothes to work. I was always early to meetings. I didn't want them to think that I followed "Indian Standard Time." I never brought Indian food for lunch. At home, before cooking, I changed out of my work clothes and covered my hair with a shower cap so I would not carry our food smells into the workplace.

Outwardly, I tried to fit in. But in terms of the actual medicine, I always thought for myself. I didn't just follow the crowd.

It was not always easy to convince people to try something new and different. First of all, I had to overcome some patients' reluctance to work with me. Some worried that they would not understand my accent. They would tell this, in my presence, to my nurse, as though I could not understand. Other times, it was my gender which was most puzzling to people. I remember one time I went in to see a new consult. The husband was in the room, and he said, "A lady doctor! Now I've seen everything." And sometimes patients hesitated to have me operate on them. A woman surgeon was quite unusual at that time, so even women patients were suspicious.

I am most proud of a treatment I introduced into the hospital: myomectomy. It is an alternative to hysterectomy. Some doctors, especially the men, are so eager to remove a woman's uterus. Every woman should be aware of myomectomy. It is a way of removing fibroid tumors while preserving the uterus. If a doctor ever tells you that you need a hysterectomy, be sure to ask about this. I was the expert at our hospital on this procedure.

I remember my first myomectomy patient. She was a single woman, about 35 years old, with fibroids. At first, I advised a hysterectomy, since that was the standard treatment. But she wanted to keep her uterus, so I did some research and discovered this alternate procedure. My chief did not want me to perform the operation. Many doctors believe that if you do not remove the entire uterus, the fibroids will return. And the chief did not understand why this woman wanted to keep her uterus. "She is never going to have a child," he said. "She isn't even married. Doesn't she know that if the uterus is removed, she will never be bothered with menstrual periods?" For him, that's all that mattered.

I performed this surgery for her. She was so grateful. She recovered, and as it happened, a year later she got married and became pregnant. I was worried about whether the uterus would function properly. I monitored her very closely. The uterus performed beautifully, and she delivered a healthy baby. I felt . . .

With one hand she flipped through the dictionary, located the word she wanted, and continued.

vindicated. I had done something a little non-standard, and it had been successful. The patient was so grateful. For years, she used to send me flowers on the child's birthday.

That first time, I did an abdominal myomectomy. Later, I learned to perform a vaginal myomectomy, in which the uterus is accessed through the cervix. It is a safer procedure which leaves no abdominal scar.

Bhagya read over her words and scratched her head.

Manisha, I don't mean to just give you medical advice. Can you understand what this meant to me?

She scanned her writing one more time. Then she capped her pen and approached the sliding glass door. She gazed beyond her patio walls at the swaying tops of the conifers, rubbing her temples with strong fingertips.

*

Saturday evening. When Manisha let herself in to her mother's condo with Charlotte in tow, it was not her mother who met her in the kitchen. Instead, an elderly white woman, her short hair like soft fur around her square face, held out a veined hand.

"Do you remember me?" The woman was an inch or so shorter than Manisha, but her commanding presence gave the impression of height.

Manisha set down her cookie sheet on the center island, grasped the hand and smiled, squinting slightly at the woman. Quiet music played in the background. It sounded vaguely Indian, with the twang of a sitar, and also airily New Age, with a woman's voice humming a melody.

"Olga?" she asked.

The woman nodded. "I was your mother's nurse for many years. So when I found out about the situation . . . " Olga raised her eyebrows, and her square hands with stubby fingers remained in the air, as though assuming Manisha could fill in the rest of the sentence.

Manisha's forehead furrowed. "It's great to see you again, Olga." She kicked off her shoes, hung up the jackets in the closet, and put a hand on Charlotte's back to urge the girl into the living room.

The house smelled of spices. Warmth emanated from the oven. "I'll just slide the samosas in to warm up," Manisha murmured. She set the timer on the stove and carried her tote bag into the living/dining area. The curtains at the sliding glass door were wide open, letting in the yellow sunset filtered through gray clouds. The concrete floor of the patio was strewn with crumpled brown leaves. From the speakers in the corner, the hollow tapping of drums beat away the seconds.

Bhagya exited the bedroom rubbing lotion onto her hands. When she saw Charlotte, she bent down, opened her arms wide and gathered the girl into them. "It has been too long since I got a hug from you," Bhagya exclaimed. "Where is your brother?"

"He was invited to a friend's house," Manisha said. "Where'd you get the music?" She strolled closer to a portable silver CD player which had been placed on the floor in a corner of the room. Its two black speakers were like the compound eyes of a giant insect.

"Olga brought it."

Manisha unzipped her bag and pulled out a tablecloth embossed with leaves. "I thought this would be good to cover up the old table."

"Fine," said Bhagya without looking at it. "Charlotte, come and help me with the plates."

Once the table had been set, everyone sat around it. "Olga brought those two," Bhagya said, pointing to the cucumber salad and a dish of creamy rice with peas. "Hungarian food. Correct?"

"My mother's recipe adapted for vegetarians. No chicken stock." Olga's voice sounded dry and crackly. Once everyone was served, Olga raised her water glass. "To my dear friend Bhagya," she said. "The best doctor I've ever worked with."

Manisha lifted her glass. Charlotte curled her fingers around her cup of juice and glanced up at Manisha, who nodded. She, too, lifted her drink in the air. Bhagya's hands remained on the tablecloth on either side of her plate.

"I'm glad you decided to have a little dinner party." Manisha smiled. The glasses clinked and beverages were sipped. "I hope you'll do this more often, now that you have time."

Bhagya's face seemed set in stone. Then she lifted her own glass. "To my best friend Olga." Her expression softened, and she trained her eyes on the woman sitting next to her. "You never forgot what your parents from Hungary taught you. I remember, when we first met, you told me, 'I know what it is like to leave everything behind and start again in a new country.' "

Once more, the drinks were lifted and lowered. Everyone, Olga included, ate their samosas, poori, and vegetable sagu with their fingers, reserving the forks for the cucumber salad and rice.

Olga cleared her throat. "Bhagya, I've always wanted to ask you this. Did you ever regret coming to this country and leaving India?"

Bhagya chewed her mouthful slowly and swallowed. "I could not have practiced medicine properly in India at that time. In the cities, we had access to some lab tests and equipment, but if you were posted to a rural area, you could not order any tests. You might not even have enough basic antibiotics." Bhagya punctured the air with her fork as she spoke. "Here in the US, I was able to practice medicine the proper way." She lowered her fork. "I am grateful for that."

"It's different in India now, though?" Manisha suggested.

"Now there are many private hospitals, in addition to government hospitals. People have a choice. So, it is better."

"Now people go to India for medical vacations!" Olga launched into a long story about a friend of hers who took the whole family to India and paid for a hip replacement, for half the cost of getting the same operation in the US.

Bhagya brushed crumbs from her fingers. "The only thing I regret is—having to raise Manisha by myself." Her gaze was directed at her plate, but she was not eating. She sat with her fingers resting on her poori.

Manisha frowned. Then she took a deep breath, leaned over, and kissed the top of Charlotte's head.

*

From her classroom doorway, Manisha supervised the students jostling at their lockers between classes. Emma, in a fuzzy bunny outfit, sashayed by. Kay, dressed in a boy's black suit and tie, pasted-on mustache, and black sunglasses, had wedged herself, with her reporter's notebook and pen, in a narrow space at the end of the hall, too narrow to fit another locker. As Emma passed her, she kicked Kay with a padded foot.

Donna, across the hall, made her way through the student traffic to Manisha.

"It's cute to see their Halloween outfits," Manisha said.

Emma clanged open the metal door of her locker, placed a red binder on the shelf inside, pulled out a blue one, and slammed the door. Kay held her notebook in front of her face, pen moving, as Emma tucked her binder and pencil pouch under one arm.

Emma edged over to stand in front of Kay.

"It looks like those two are getting to be friends," Donna remarked.

"Hey!" Kay shouted.

Emma pranced away and hurried through a doorway behind a robot in a foil-covered cardboard box.

Kay's pen dropped from her fingers. She turned and set her

forehead against the back wall.

"I spoke too soon," Donna murmured. "I'll go see what's wrong."

*

"I'm going to ask you to speak to Kay." Pauline stood beside Manisha's desk. The wind whistled outside the sealed-shut windows, and the fluorescent lights overhead cast a cold brightness over the brushed-metal bookshelves. "I've got Emma in my office. She's admitted to taking Kay's notebook. Kay allowed me to see the notebook, but it appears that she's writing in some sort of code. She doesn't want to tell me what it's all about. She seems to like you, so I thought—"

"I'd be happy to." Manisha stood and straightened the ID badge clipped to her blazer.

Pauline strode to the door on her low-heeled boots and re-entered with Kay trailing behind her, clutching her journal to her chest. The girl had taken off her sunglasses and mustache. Manisha smiled and patted a space at one of the round tables. Kay took a seat, setting her notebook on the table. She was so short that her heels did not quite reach the floor. Pauline exited, closing the door behind her.

Manisha, seated next to Kay, re-adjusted the scarf around her neck. "Can I see?" She pointed at the notebook. Kay pushed it towards her. Manisha lifted the cover. The pages were filled with writing in what looked like capital letters interspersed with symbols.

"Do you know the Cyrillic alphabet?" Kay asked.

"Is that what Russian is written in?"

Kay swung her legs under the table. "It's easy. My dad showed me. He's a professor of Russian literature."

Manisha ran a finger over the letters.

"And my mom's a professor of mathematics. I've inherited both, because I'm good at math and languages." Kay stretched her mouth into a Cheshire-cat grin.

Manisha nodded. "Tell me what you have here."

"Some of the letters look like English letters, but they have a different sound. This one looks like an H, but the sound is like N. And this one looks like a P, but it sounds like an R. Except you have to roll it." Kay demonstrated, her tongue fluttering in her mouth.

"You're good at that," Manisha said.

"For my name, you use a K, like in English. But there's no letter to sound like 'ay' in Russian, so I have to use a short E sound, plus a long E sound, like this." She pointed to a word that looked like "KEN," but with a backwards capital N.

"So . . . are you writing in Russian? Do you know Russian?"

"I'm writing in English with the Russian alphabet. It's a code. I don't want to get caught, like Harriet did."

"Harriet?"

"Harriet the Spy. Other kids found her notebook, and she got in big trouble. But I figure the kids in this school are too stupid to crack my code." Kay kicked rhythmically at the table leg.

Manisha frowned at the rows of symbols. "Do you want to tell me what it says on this page?"

Kay shook her head.

Manisha rested an elbow on the table and leaned towards Kay. "Do you know why Emma took your notebook?"

Kay tucked her hands under her thighs. "I'm just writing stuff down. Aliya likes me to do that."

"Aliya has asked you to, kind of, spy on people?"

Kay wiggled her feet up and down. She started to nod. Then she hung her head and peered at her knees.

"I think your friends are upset because they don't know what you're writing. You're being secretive."

Kay wrinkled her nose.

"It's hard to be friends with people if you're keeping secrets from them." Manisha tilted her head. "Would it be OK if I took this home over the weekend and tried to figure it out?"

Kay sighed. "I guess."

*

The front door was open, and through the glass storm door a large jack-o'-lantern could be seen on the front porch, flame flickering in its grin. Inside, the house was dim. Orange candles burned on the dining table. Manisha, a black cape draped over her sweater, held up a hat with panda ears and eyes.

"Are you going to take away my hard and sticky candy again?" Charlotte, dressed in a white and black fuzzy outfit, closed her eyes as Manisha slipped the panda hat over her short hair, fastening the flaps under her chin.

"I'll give you ten cents for each one, just like I did last year." Manisha patted the round panda ears.

"But I'm older this year! I should get to keep all my candy."

"Hard candy rots your teeth. Chocolate is better." Manisha handed Charlotte an orange candy pail and opened the storm door. The fall air, smelling of wood fires, chilled her face. "Daddy's waiting outside. Go on."

Manisha closed the storm door and watched the panda walk away, holding hands with a tall white man. She positioned a folding chair near the doorway, set a bowl of mini chocolate bars next to it, and sat down with Kay's notebook on her knee. She thumbed over the screen of her phone to open a site called "Russian for Everyone."

NOVEMBER

Before school started for the day, Manisha sat with Kay again at one of the round tables in her classroom. In front of her was Kay's closed reporter's notebook.

"Kay, I managed to translate some of your code." She flipped up the cover to reveal a half sheet of paper in her own writing. "Here's what I think is on the first page." She unclipped the sheet and pushed it over to Kay.

Kay read:

Emma's hair is the color of mud.
Aliya is so bossy.
Izzie is dumb.
Maria thinks she's white and normal.
That new girl is ugly. She's so dark.
Emma's braces make her breath stinky.

Kay's breathing grew heavier. She reached for her notebook, but Manisha scooted it away, keeping her fingertips on it. She retrieved the translation and folded it in fourths. "Kay, I'm concerned about what you've written. Do you know why?"

"They can't figure out my code, so what does it matter?" Kay pouted.

Manisha flipped through the pages. "You've been spending your time secretly writing negative things about your friends. Are they really your friends?"

Kay's head hung so low that her nose almost touched the table.

"I'm going to suggest some things to you. First of all, I'd like your permission to throw this notebook away."

Kay's head shot up. "No!"

"The other alternative is that I will keep it and show it to your parents at the parent-teacher conference coming up. I'm sure your father won't have any trouble deciphering it."

From Kay's drooping head, a tear splashed to the table.

"What would you prefer? Should I throw it away? Or show it to your parents?"

"Throw it away," Kay said in a small voice.

"Good decision." Manisha slipped the notebook onto her lap. "And I'm also going to suggest that you find some new friends, since you don't seem to like these girls very much. Are there other kids you do like?"

Kay shook her head. Her black hair swung over her face.

"Nirali could probably use another friend."

"Fiona was her summer buddy."

"That's true. You could be friends with Fiona and Nirali."

Kay wrinkled her nose. "I don't like them."

"Why not?"

"Emma doesn't like Fiona. She thinks Fiona is babyish."

"Why does it matter what Emma thinks?"

"She'll make fun of me if I become friends with Fiona."

Manisha sighed. "What about Nirali?"

"She's from a different country."

"She's just as American as you are."

"I'm a real American because my parents were born in America."

Manisha drummed her fingers on the cover of Kay's notebook. "What about me? Am I a real American?"

Kay shrugged. "You're a teacher."

"Kay. Listen to me. You're going to have to expand your idea of friendship. It sounds like you're so afraid that people will make fun of you that you're spying on them to make sure they don't."

Kay kicked the toe of her sneaker at the table leg.

"Today at lunch I'll look for you. I want to see you sitting with someone new. It doesn't have to be Nirali or Fiona, but I want to see you working on making some different friends. Would you be willing to try that?"

Kay stood up. "Can I go now?"

*

Dear Manisha,

In looking over what I've written, I wonder if you will think I am bragging. I would like you to know the truth about me. I would like you to know that I have not always done the right thing.

When your father died, his family wanted me to come back to India. That is the custom: when the husband dies, the in-laws must take care of his wife and children. Perhaps I should have listened. Perhaps I should have raised you in India, surrounded by grandparents and aunts.

But I had worked so hard to build my career. In India at that time, most of the hospitals were government-owned. There was so much corruption, and no oversight. No standards. Patients had to pray they were lucky enough to be seen by a conscientious doctor. And at the hospitals, the pay for doctors was so low. If you wanted to get along, you had to accept money under the table. I was not interested in that. Maybe I could have established a private practice in Bangalore. I know of doctors who became wealthy this way. You had to be . . . You must only accept patients who can pay.

In any case, I wanted you to have the advantage of an American education. So, I stayed here and raised you on my own. Was it the right decision? I can never know.

*

A Thanksgiving potluck was arranged on the kitchen counters of a renovated farmhouse: slices of turkey, gravy, stuffing, cranberry sauce, romaine lettuce salad, wild rice pilaf, mashed potatoes, sautéed green beans, and a variety of baked goods. Among these traditional dishes: a platter of fried pakodas with a jar of bright green chutney next to it.

"Thanks for having us over. As usual." Manisha balanced a plate of food on her palm as she stood in the kitchen.

Lee Ann wiped a spill of juice from the counter. "You're family. It wouldn't be Thanksgiving without you." She was a petite white woman with shoulder-length hair and a face scored with laugh lines. A pink apron was tied over her pink sweater.

Manisha leaned back against the counter between the stove and sink. The inside of the house had been remodeled in a modern, open design. Lee Ann's children and their cousins surrounded the dining table on the other side of the kitchen island and, past them, Manisha could see into the living room, where her mother sat next to Lee Ann's mother. "If it weren't for you, we probably would never celebrate Thanksgiving, since Mom ignores all holidays."

"It must've been painful for her to celebrate without your dad." Lee Ann rinsed the sponge.

"Either that, or she didn't care about anything except her work."

Lee Ann glanced at Bhagya as she untied her apron and lifted it over her head. "Your mother is a courageous doctor."

"I guess you know more about her work life than I do, since you're a nurse." Manisha speared a few green beans.

"How's school going?" Lee Ann picked up a plate and began serving herself.

"My boss seems very happy with me so far." Manisha nibbled at a green bean. "I'm not sure I'm having a big impact as a role model, though. One of my students was adopted from China as a baby, and she's struggling with identity issues. But she won't really allow me to help her. She just sees me as a teacher."

"Your presence in the school is important, I'm sure."

"For the past few weeks Kay's been either sitting alone at lunch, or on the edge of her former group of friends. She's so afraid of what people will think of her that she's paralyzed in terms of making new friends."

"Those kids are lucky to have you as their teacher. Just the fact that you care, that you're paying attention."

Manisha stirred her wild rice. "I don't know, Lee Ann. I feel like I'm not helping her at all."

*

Bhagya shifted her seat to be near Lee Ann's husband, Lyle. "I would like to ask you a question." She wore a cardigan and blouse over knit jeans. Her plate, filled with vegetables and baked goods, balanced on her lap.

With his large cleft chin and brown puppy-dog eyes, Lyle looked like the cartoon Dudley Do-Right. "I'm all ears." He inserted a forkful of turkey and gravy into his mouth.

"I would like to know the process of getting a letter to the editor published."

Lyle swallowed while pressing a paper napkin to his lips. "There's an online form on our web site that you can use. Or you can just send it to me, and I can forward it to the right person. What's your letter about?"

"I have not written it yet." Bhagya poked at her mashed potatoes. "How likely is it that my letter would be published?"

"The most important thing is to respond to a recent article. Make sure your letter makes a clear point, and is not too long.

Two hundred words max, which is about 2/3 of a typed page. And include your name, address, phone number."

"I see." Bhagya spread green chutney over her mashed potatoes. "So, you do not publish letters of general interest which are not responses to a recent article?"

"I'm not saying we never would, but you'd have a better chance if you're reacting to something we've just published. I'd be happy to look over a draft if you like."

Bhagya shook her head. "Thank you. That will not be necessary."

DECEMBER

"Close your eyes." Manisha, holding a paper grocery sack, smiled at the roomful of sixth graders. Spiral-bound notebooks were open in front of each student on the round tables.

Izzie squeezed her eyes shut. Wilson closed his, opened them, looked around the room, closed them, and opened them again. One student glanced at the clock near the doorway. The second hand jerked along silently. 8:15 and 33 seconds. 8:15 and 34 seconds.

"Why?" Aliya asked. She opened her brown eyes wide.

"Close your eyes and hold out your hand," Manisha said. "I'll give each of you an object. Feel it first. See if it makes a sound. Smell it. Don't taste it."

"Aww!" several kids moaned.

"Don't taste it," Manisha repeated. "Then, without opening your eyes, jot some words in your journal."

"How can we write with our eyes closed?" Emma's braces flashed around the room. A few kids giggled.

"You can do it." Manisha shifted the bag to her left hand. "Just write words. Then after one minute, I'll tell you to open your eyes, and you'll keep writing for four more minutes."

Hands flailed in the air and mouths opened.

"Are we all getting the same thing?"

"What if I don't know what my object is?"

"What if I can't write with my eyes closed?"

"Why are we doing this?"

Manisha held one arm straight up. "Fiona has her hand raised silently." She nodded at a girl with hair so straight and silky that the tops of her ears poked through, giving her an elf-like appearance. "Go ahead, Fiona."

Fiona's arm descended slowly. She frowned at her shoes. "I forget."

Manisha raised the bag of objects. "This is a warm-up exercise to help us include more sensory detail in our writing."

"Plus, it'll be fun!" Wilson exclaimed, eyes open and hands out.

Izzie, lids still screwed shut, held out a hand, fingers wiggling. "Me first!"

All the students closed their eyes. Some cupped their palms on the table. Some stretched their arms out full-length. "Me first! Me first!"

"The quiet students get an object," Manisha said.

The room fell silent. Manisha crept along, placing an offering into each student's waiting hand.

*

Manisha stood on a stepstool in her kitchen to reach a large plastic container on a high shelf. As she set the container on the counter next to the half-empty pan of burritos, her eyes fell on an almost invisible object in the back corner of the cabinet. She reached in. Her fingers curved around cool glass, and as she stepped down the stool, she clutched a transparent cylinder to her chest.

Her feet on the ground, she set the footed glass hurricane candleholder on the counter. Its rim was edged with silver. Etched on the side were the words "Manisha and Gerard, June 21, 2000." She climbed back up, felt around on the top shelf, and came down with a beeswax pillar candle, its wick fresh, its wax undisturbed.

She finished putting away the leftovers. The dishwasher hummed and sloshed rhythmically. She wiped the gray granite counters and the stainless-steel surface of the stove.

Then, carrying the candle in its holder and a box of matches, she climbed the stairs to her bedroom. One side of the king bed was covered with books, notebooks, and her closed laptop. She set the candleholder on the sill of the bow window near her desk and struck a match to the wick. She watched as the flame blossomed and the wax around it began to soften.

After arranging the pillows into a backrest, she pulled a notebook from the pile on the bed and began writing. Half an hour later, after some crossing out and re-writing, she had this:

Solstice Light

I tend the candle in
the etched glass holder,
a wedding present,
a gift we never used.
For years on a shelf, now
aglow on the windowsill.
You are not here to see it.
The beeswax candle smells sweet as
clover on a summer day.
Our wedding day was the first day of summer.
Tonight, the flame flickers
against snow outside,

the first night of winter.
When the flame drowns
in wax, in my tears,
I pour out the warm honey-
scented liquid
and the flame leaps,
strong and free.

The sky outside the window was dark, and no snow had
fallen. The flame burned on black glass.

*

Dear Manisha,

*Let me tell you one more story about a regret. As a doctor,
I never liked performing abortions. There was no challenge
with the early terminations, which are the most common. But
I have always agreed that women should have access to safe
abortions, so I offered this procedure to my patients for that
reason.*

*Once, after a procedure, I tried to give some advice. The
patient was a college student. This was her second unplanned
pregnancy. She was not reliable about birth control. So I said
to her, "You are young. You have your whole life ahead of
you. Why don't you concentrate on studying now, and worry
about boys later, after you have your degree and you are
ready to marry?"*

*She did not appreciate my effort. She sat there in her paper
gown and looked me in the eye and said: "I don't take advice
from women with mustaches."*

Manisha, you know Indian women sometimes have dark-

er skin or thin hair on our upper lip. I had never thought anything of it before. It was never an issue. And here this youngster was insulting me. Her doctor. Her elder. The person who had made it possible for her to continue her education without the interruption of a baby. I was so shocked. An Indian young woman in a similar situation would be dying of shame, she would be crying, and here this white woman was coolly tossing insults at me.

After that, I never bothered to give that kind of advice to any Americans. I did not bother about their personal lives. I just took care of their bodies. That is what Americans want, isn't it? Privacy. They don't want foreigners telling them what to do.

But I consider this a failing of mine. I did not find a way to truly connect with these young women.

I did not find a way to truly connect with you, either.

JANUARY

Manisha sat on the sofa in her mother's condo. "What is it that you wanted my help with?"

"I have been writing about my life." Bhagya patted the yellow legal pad on her lap. "And . . . there is something that happened recently. I would like to make my actions known . . . to the people. To the public. I thought I should tell my life story, but now . . . I want to write something short and to the point. You are talented at writing. I wonder if you would help."

"Is this about . . . what happened to you at work? Why they asked you to retire?"

Bhagya rubbed the veins on the back of one hand with the thumb of the other hand. She turned her head away from Manisha and looked at the framed photo on the table: teenaged Manisha in her prom dress. She sighed. "I am not sure you will understand."

"I'm not in high school anymore, Mom."

Bhagya interlaced her fingers on her legal pad. She folded her lips inward. "Have you ever made a decision"—she coughed once— "that you knew, without a doubt, was the right decision, but which was disapproved of by many others?"

"Many others?" Manisha echoed. "I've made decisions that you didn't approve of."

"I mean, decisions that society as a whole . . . many people in society—"

"No." Manisha shook her head. "I wouldn't do that."

"I see." Bhagya held herself still for a moment. Then, she turned to the sliding glass doors.

Manisha followed her mother's gaze. A blue jay had alighted on the snow-topped privacy wall of the patio. Its clean white shirt shone in the sunlight.

"I like to look at the birds," Bhagya said quietly. "Sometimes I will just sit here and watch."

The jay outside opened its black beak and emitted a stuttering, creaking call.

"So, Mom. Are you going to tell me what happened, or not?"

"I have Alzheimer's."

"You have what?"

"Alzheimer's. The medical director was right." Bhagya's gaze remained out the window.

"You mean, the man who asked you to leave?" Manisha stared at her mother's ear.

Bhagya nodded. Her hands were still clasped in her lap, pressing into the legal pad.

"How did . . . have you seen a doctor?"

"Two doctors. Two different doctors. I went to Indianapolis last week. I did not want to see anyone around here. Too many people know me." Bhagya cleared her throat. "Doctors are supposed to keep patient information confidential, but we are human. They would talk. Everyone would come to know."

"You drove there yourself? Why didn't you ask me to take you?"

"An acquaintance took me."

"An acquaintance? Who?"

Bhagya shook her head. "I want to keep her name con . . . a secret," she said. "This woman has family in Indianapolis, so she did not mind. I did not tell her my reasons. I just asked her to drop me off and pick me up."

"And you didn't tell me."

"I wanted to be by myself. So, I went, and they did the tests."

The clock above the fireplace chimed on the hour. The two of them sat still as the bell sounded three times.

Manisha slid an inch closer to her mother on the sofa. "Are you sure?" Her mother had not turned around. "I've heard there is no definitive test for Alzheimer's."

"There is no blood test." Bhagya flipped to the back pages of her legal pad. "I have written it all here. They did a complete physical. They tested my blood for . . . low blood sugar, urinary tract infection." She scanned her list with an index finger. "They had me take some mental status tests. And they did a brain scan. The scan showed quite a bit . . . quite a bit of . . ." she consulted her list— "deterioration. The doctors said I have been able to function well because I am . . . because I have . . . I've gone to school a lot. Because I am a doctor." She flipped the legal pad closed and sat up very straight, with her hands clutched together in her lap. She looked like an impenetrable statue.

"You may have many years left." Manisha reached towards her mother, and then stopped and clamped her own hands together.

Out the window, the blue jay had flown away. Several small brown sparrows fluttered around the feeder. Bhagya licked her dry lips. "That is what the doctors said. And I know the drill. They say these things because no one knows for sure. I may progress very quickly."

The faint roar of an airplane increased in volume and pitch overhead. Both women looked up at the ceiling, and kept their gaze there as the sound descended and faded.

Manisha dropped her eyes and caught her mother's. "Mom. I'm here for you. I'll take care of you. Don't worry."

"You don't understand doctors." Bhagya turned away, squinting out at the birds. "You don't understand hospitals. They take control. We take control. I used to do this, too. The patient is an object that we diagnose and try to manipulate. Our aim is to keep them alive at all costs. If the patient dies, we feel we have lost the game. They—the doctors—do not want to give up control."

Manisha inhaled sharply, as though she hadn't breathed in many minutes.

"I have seen doctors ignore living wills and patient directives, especially if the relatives are not sure. Once you present yourself to the hospital, you cannot start refusing treatment. The doctors, even the sensitive ones, have to follow a certain . . . certain rules." Bhagya's speech was loud and labored. "So, once you put yourself in their hands, you have lost control. I have seen doctors treat pneumonia in patients with dementia. I have seen a doctor put a . . . the thing they put in your heart to regulate . . ." Bhagya patted her chest over her heart.

"Pace—"

"Pacemaker. I have seen them put this in an old woman with Alzheimer's. This woman did not even know who she was. She could do nothing for herself. This woman had a living will, but it only applied to a . . . an illness where you are going to die soon. A terminal illness. Alzheimer's is not considered terminal. The deterioration can be slow. The woman's daughter was upset and could not give a clear answer. So, the doctors took control."

Manisha's eyes were clouded with tears.

Bhagya turned towards her daughter and reached for Manisha's hands. "You are a good daughter. I have not been a good mother to you."

Manisha, tears streaming down her face, allowed Bhagya to grasp her hands. Her mother's grip was dry and firm.

*

Every morning as she left for work, and every afternoon before she got into her car, Manisha scanned the sky. Most of the time, it was white with clouds. She saw few birds, and no hawks.

FEBRUARY

"As you all know, Grandparents' Day is next Friday." Pauline stood in the auditorium, her padded shoulders and gray-haired head rising above the top of the lectern. Her manicured hands shuffled through a stack of papers. The screen behind her displayed the mascot of Newton School, a rocket in red and gold. Below the stage, Pauline's secretary, willowy Jessica, stood in front of a cart with a laptop. Faculty from the entire school perched in the dimness on rows of padded seats.

"This is a major fundraiser for our school, and I know you will all do everything you can to make the grandparents feel welcome and special."

After reviewing the schedule for Grandparents Day, Pauline scanned the crowd of teachers for a few seconds. "You've all sent me your proposals for your classes, which I have here." She waved the sheaf of papers. "I'll want to talk to some of you right after this meeting. But I'm sure I don't need to remind all of you that any props, costumes, and supplies need to be prepared ahead of time. Remember, this event is designed to impress the grandparents and let them know that their students are receiving an education that they can't get anywhere else except right here at Newton. Now, let me read the names of the teachers who should see me after this meeting."

Teachers began shuffling into the aisles. Several approached Pauline as she stepped down from the stage. Jessica, her long blond hair cascading around her, was bending and straightening, unplugging the laptop and turning off the projector.

"What're you planning for Grandparents' Day?" Donna asked Manisha as they walked out of the dark auditorium into the fluorescent-bright hallway.

"The kids have read a novel called *Swami and Friends*, which is by R.K. Narayan, a famous Indian author," Manisha said. "And—"

Donna stopped in the middle of the hallway. "Shouldn't you be somewhere else?" A few boys in athletic shorts and enormous shoes sat around on basketballs next to the boys' locker room. She raised her eyebrows at them.

"We're waiting for Darnell. He takes forever getting dressed."

"He doesn't need you to wait for him. Go ahead to the gym." She made shooing motions with her hands. "And no dribbling in the hallway."

The boys tucked the balls under their arms and loped away.

In the silent hallway, Manisha and Donna stopped at the doorway to Donna's classroom. "You were telling me?" Donna smiled in a tired way at Manisha.

Manisha unclipped her name badge. "Each class chose a scene from the novel and created a skit."

Donna stepped into her doorway. "Pauline approved it?"

"She didn't call my name to meet with her, so I assume it's fine. What are you doing?"

"My kids write two-person poems every January, and we always perform them for Grandparents' Day."

"That sounds fun."

"I'm sure your skits will be a big hit." Donna smiled and disappeared into her classroom.

*

Manisha, long hair in a ponytail, squatted on the plush wool rug of Lee Ann's living room, wrapping a long white piece of gold-bordered cotton cloth around Charlotte's waist. Charlotte giggled and squirmed. Lee Ann, a pink bandana over her dark hair, leaned against the doorway between the living room and dining room. Her daughter Lani ran around the dining table, already wearing her dhoti, which looked like a loose, pleated pair of trousers. The house smelled warm and sweet.

"You learned to wrap these from YouTube?" Lee Ann asked.

"My mom kept my father's dhotis all these years, but she had no idea how to wear them." Manisha made narrow pleats in one end of the cloth. "Stand still, Charlotte." She stood up to tuck the pleats into the cloth at the waist. "Fortunately, I only have two dhotis. I don't think I'd have the patience to wrap these on a whole classroom of kids."

"And this is how the boys dressed back then? When was it?"

Manisha tugged and smoothed the dhoti. "About 1930 or 1931. We watched some video clips from an Indian TV show based on this book, and this is what most of the boys wore. Try walking around, Charlotte."

Charlotte strutted back and forth. The pleats of the fabric bobbed with each step.

Manisha stood up, flipping her ponytail back over her shoulder. "Looks good. Does it feel secure around your waist?"

Charlotte jumped in place. "It's not falling down."

Lani skipped up, tagged Charlotte, and said, "Let's go to my room!"

"Let me take off the dhotis first." Manisha grabbed for the nearest girl and unwrapped the fabric.

"Do you girls want muffins?" Lee Ann asked.

"Later!" Lani yelled as they clambered up the stairs.

Once the girls were out of the way, the two women sat in the kitchen on high stools, their coffee mugs on the breakfast bar in front of them. A pan of muffins cooled on a wooden trivet.

"This novel was perfect for my sixth-graders," Manisha said. "Swami and his friends are about the same age as my students, and the kids could really relate to all the friendship drama. I'm worried about Izzie, though. She's making no effort to memorize her lines, and when I sent home an e-mail, I got no response."

Lee Ann lifted two muffins out of the pan and onto two plates. She pushed one over to Manisha. "How's your mom doing these days?" Lee Ann's forehead creased.

"I can't believe she has Alzheimer's. She must have misinterpreted the tests, or misunderstood what the doctors said."

Lee Ann considered her muffin as she peeled away the paper wrapper. "Your mom's always been a smart woman."

"And she's still smart." Manisha broke off the toasted top of the muffin. "She's already made plans for my birthday dinner next month. Remember when I was a kid, and she'd sometimes forget my birthday?"

Lee Ann folded her paper wrapper. "I think it was when you were in fifth or sixth grade, you were so mad at your mom that you threw your own un-birthday party a month later at our house, and you wouldn't let her come over."

"It was fifth grade. You helped me make a cake." Manisha bit into her muffin and shielded her mouth with her hand as she spoke. "I think she's doing really well. Maybe the stress of the retirement and the move . . . but she'll adjust soon."

Lee Ann put a hand on Manisha's shoulder. "Let me know if you need any help."

*

The classroom was packed with rows of folding chairs, on which were seated wrinkled guests. The round tables from the classroom had been moved into the hallway, where nervous kids stood in costume. Manisha paced down the row of students. Several of them wore white paper Gandhi caps which looked somewhat like a baker's skull cap.

Aliya raised her hand. "Ms. V, I have a protest." Her long brown hair was braided and coiled around her head. She wore dress pants and a tie.

"What do you want to protest?" Manisha smiled down at the girl.

"All the characters in this book are boys, so the girls have to dress up as boys. I don't think that's fair."

"You make a good point," Manisha said. "Next year—"

"Next year you should choose a book with all girls," Aliya said, "so the boys have to dress up as girls."

Several girls giggled. A few boys groaned. "No way I'm dressing up as a girl," one boy said.

"Are you planning to fail?" Emma asked.

"What d'you mean?"

"We'll be in seventh grade next year. So, it'll be this year's fifth-graders who have to—"

"Then I think it's a great idea!" the boy declared.

Manisha stopped in front of Wilson. Her eyebrows contracted. He stood upright, shoulders back, in his sandals, dhoti, button-down shirt, and Gandhi cap. Between his eyebrows was a splotch of red.

"What's that on your forehead, Wilson?" Manisha asked.

"You know how on the video clip, Swami put on that red powder after praying?"

"Kumkum."

"Yeah. That stuff."

She touched a fingertip to the red smear and then examined her finger. "What did you use?"

"Marker!"

Manisha frowned. "I'm not sure . . ."

"I wanted to look authentic. I'm the main character!"

Manisha sighed and stepped back. "Everyone ready?"

Heads nodded.

"I'll introduce the novel, and then we'll start the skit."

*

Several students sat on a narrow bench under the interactive white board. They elbowed each other and threw bits of paper into the air. Fiona entered, and the students immediately stopped clowning around and stood up. "Good morning, teacher," they said in unison.

Fiona wore a business suit and a large cross pendant on her chest. She carried a heavy book covered in white paper, with the word "Bible" written in large letters on the spine and front. She took her place at a lectern and opened the book on its slanted surface. The students sat down.

"This is our Moral Values class," Fiona said. "Today I will read to you from the Bible about the time Jesus healed the sick." She looked down at the book and read. "'When Jesus came down from the hill, great crowds followed him. Then a man with a skin disease came to Jesus. The man bowed down before him and said, "Lord, you can heal me if you will." Jesus reached out his hand and touched the man and said, "I will. Be healed!" And immediately the man was healed from his disease.'" Fiona looked up. "You should all become Christians. Can your stone images heal the sick?" She came out from behind the lectern and raised a fist. "No! They are dirty, worthless idols. Can they talk? Can they take you to heaven? You must believe in Jesus. He is the son of God."

Wilson stood up. "If Jesus was the son of God, why did he eat meat and drink wine?" He spoke loudly, grinning and looking into the audience at his grandparents.

The grandfather sat with a large fist on each thigh. The grandmother, ankles crossed under her chair, tilted her knees towards her husband.

Fiona waved her arms around in anger. She approached Wilson and mock-slapped him.

"Ow!" Wilson held his palm to his cheek and glared at Fiona. "I'll tell my father that you hurt me!"

All the students except Wilson dispersed out the door, carrying the bench with them. Nothing happened for a few seconds. Manisha hurried to the classroom door, opened it, and beckoned to Izzie, who entered. She was dressed in long pants and a button-down shirt. She carried a pen and a legal pad. As soon as she approached the "stage" area, Wilson ran to her. "Father! The scripture teacher said bad things about our gods and slapped me in class today!"

Izzie scribbled on the tablet. "Take this letter to your headmaster." She ripped the paper from the pad and held it out to Wilson.

Wilson held the paper and stared at it. "Father, I'm scared to go to the headmaster."

"You must. The teachers should not treat Hindu students like this. I will send . . ." Izzie looked around, bewildered. Manisha stepped to her and whispered in her ear.

"I could send you to a different school," Izzie said. She stood silent. Manisha motioned with her hand, and Izzie left the room.

Izzie's grandfather gripped the head of his cane as his eyes followed his granddaughter out the door.

Several boys, along with Fiona and Aliya, entered. Aliya stood as tall as she could, smoothed her tie over her shirt, and thrust her chin in the air. She carried the same legal pad and pen that Izzie had just used.

Wilson cowered in a corner of the room with his sheet of paper. The other boys tried to push him towards Aliya. "You have to give the letter to the headmaster," one boy said.

Finally, Wilson was propelled by his friends. He thrust his letter at Aliya, who glanced at the paper and looked up at Fiona. "You must respect all religions," she said.

Fiona looked at the floor. "I'm sorry, sir."

"Swami, in the future, you do not need to go to your father for things like this. You should come to me first." She scribbled on the legal pad, and ripped off a page. She handed it to Wilson with a flourish. "Take this letter of apology to your father."

Wilson held up the letter with a smile. The boys clapped Wilson on the back in congratulations.

Manisha let out her breath. All the students stood in a row, smiling at the audience, which applauded politely. Wilson ran to his grandparents. His grandmother put her fingers under his chin, took out a tissue, and wiped at his forehead, but the red mark remained. Izzie's grandfather, leaning on his cane, gazed around the room, frowning slightly, as she chattered and giggled.

MARCH

"Thanks for inviting me out for my birthday." Manisha sipped her white wine. They sat on deeply padded chairs at a low table. Multicolored globes of lamps hung in the dim air scented with warm bread and savory spices.

"Manisha, I am not good at apologizing. But I am sorry that, when you were a child, I did not give you the celebrations you liked."

Manisha shook her head. "It's OK, Mom. I know that birthdays were no big deal in India."

"When I was growing up, we had so many Hindu holidays. And in those days most families had three or four children at least, so we didn't bother about each one's birthday. But you are my only child. I should have—"

"Don't worry about it, Mom." Manisha arranged her cloth napkin over her lap. "How long has it been since you ate out?"

"When I was working, I was too busy to socialize."

"I think you just enjoyed cooking. Even when your relatives came to visit, you'd spend hours in the kitchen."

"This is one thing I regret. I took you to India only once. I did not make much effort to visit my cousins in North America. So, you see them all as 'my relatives.' They are yours, too. I will give you their addresses. You must keep in touch. If not for your sake, then for the sake of your children."

"They've got their father's family. Lots of cousins on that side. So, how've you been recently?"

Bhagya took a gulp of water and crunched on the ice cubes.

"It's so quiet in the house. I didn't realize how much work filled up my life. You used to accuse me of . . . of only caring about my work, and I never believed it. You used to tell me that I had no hobbies. And now I am wondering if you were right. Sometimes I do not know what to do with myself."

Her mother murmured these last words, and Manisha had to strain to hear over the background din.

The server deposited a platter of oil-drizzled hummus, chopped salad, and lavosh bread.

"Now is the perfect time to develop a hobby, Mom. What are your interests?" Manisha ripped off a piece of the soft, flat bread and dabbed it in the hummus.

"Medicine was my interest. Now . . . I don't know. I have nothing."

"What about your writing?"

Bhagya spread a piece of lavosh with hummus, sprinkled it with chopped salad, and rolled it into a cylinder. "When I read over what I've written, I'm not sure if I am communicating what I really want to say. The writing is more difficult than I thought it would be."

Manisha frowned. "If you just want to write about your life . . . maybe I could help you."

"Perhaps it is because of my training. My mentor, Dr. Harold Williams, used to tell me, 'Bhagya, you must make the best medical decision you can, based on all the knowledge you have, and then forget about it. Don't keep thinking about your decision all night.' So, it is not in my nature to look back." Bhagya bit the end of her cylinder, chewed meditatively, and swallowed. "I will look to the future, and not the past."

Manisha attempted a smile. "That sounds like a very positive attitude."

The candle on the table flickered and the lamps around them glinted. When the waiter took away the appetizer plate,

Bhagya zipped open her purse and extracted a small box with a tiny rose-shaped bow on top. "This is for you. Happy birthday."

Manisha cradled the box in cupped hands. "Mom, you didn't have to—"

Bhagya's lips smiled, but her eyes seemed sad. "Open it."

Manisha carefully pulled open the wrapping paper. Inside was a ring box. She lifted the top. An oval sky-blue stone gleamed between two round glittering diamonds. Manisha gasped. "It's lovely."

"If it doesn't fit, we can get it resized."

Manisha pinched it from its velvet cushion. It fit perfectly on the ring finger of her right hand. She tilted it back and forth to allow the stones to catch the light. "Thank you so much, Mom. I never expected anything like this."

"I wanted you to have something beautiful from me."

Manisha stood, leaned over the table, and hugged her mother awkwardly. A server waited for her to re-seat herself, and then set two plates down: rice pilaf with sautéed vegetables, and spanakopita. The scents of baked pastry, garlic and mint wafted around the table.

"How is your job going?" Bhagya cut a portion from her spanakopita and transferred it to the edge of her daughter's plate.

Manisha blinked rapidly down at her plate with her mother's offering. She looked at the ring, and at the diamond bracelet on her wrist. She took a deep breath. "Very well, I think." She cleared her throat. "You want some of this?"

"I will try it."

Manisha scooped some rice and vegetables and conveyed them to her mother's plate. "I've had parents tell me that their kids are reading more, and noticing vocabulary words on the news."

"So, you managed to wrap those dhotis?"

"The kids looked really cute."

"How did the grandparents feel about the skits?"

"Some of them thanked me afterwards. They seemed to enjoy the performances."

"I am very glad to hear that."

Manisha lifted a forkful of pilaf. "Fortunately, things are different now, Mom, than they were when you first came to this country."

*

Pauline removed her glasses and moved to a seat at the table in her office. Manisha, already at the table, smiled and picked up her pen. The lines under Pauline's eyes were prominent. She folded her glasses and placed them on the table in front of her.

"Manisha, I hate to tell you this, but I'm afraid it's just not working out."

Manisha's smile dropped. Her forehead creased. "You mean, there's something wrong with my teaching?"

Pauline nodded.

"What is it? What am I doing wrong?"

Pauline reached for her glasses and brought them into her lap. "You don't have good control of the classroom. The last time I observed, you were shushing the kids an awful lot."

"The kids disagreed about the persuasive essay we were reading, so they—"

"You need to plan for that kind of thing."

"I had no idea they'd get so worked up about it."

"Exactly." Pauline smiled. "You need to do a better job of predicting their responses."

"I understand. But that doesn't seem like such a big deal. I mean, at least they were engaged with what we were reading.

That seems more important to me."

Pauline touched the endpiece of her glasses to the corner of her mouth. "Are you arguing with me?"

"No, of course not."

"Your voice is quite loud."

"I'm sorry." Manisha moved her hands from the table to her lap, and cast her eyes down.

"And Manisha, it's not just your classroom control. We've had complaints from parents."

"Which parents? I'd be happy to meet with them and work things out."

Pauline tilted her head. A small, sympathetic smile played on her lips. "It's confidential, I'm afraid."

Manisha frowned down at the stack of folders. "Is there anything I can do to make it right for them?"

"I'm afraid not."

"So." Manisha ran a thumb down the tabs of the folders. "You're saying that I won't get a contract for next year."

"I'm so sorry."

She lifted her eyes to Pauline and opened the top folder. "I thought you wanted to look at some student portfolios. They've done great work." She picked up a typed paper.

"That won't be necessary now."

Manisha held the paper in the air for a moment. Then she set it down and closed the folder. "Was it Izzie's parents? Because I sent them an e-mail about her failing grades?"

"We'll give you a very good recommendation." Pauline set her glasses on the top of her head and leaned forward on her forearms. "And, for your own sake, Manisha, I would advise you to let people know that this was your decision."

Manisha blinked at Pauline.

"I assume you can go back to the university."

"I've really enjoyed teaching middle school."

"In that case, you might consider getting your teaching license, so you'll have more options."

"Is that what the complaint was about? That I don't have a teaching license?"

Pauline sat back in her chair. Her gaze drifted to the window. Pale late afternoon sunshine washed into the room.

"I understood that a license was not required to teach at this school, since it's a private school." Manisha's voice had grown unsteady.

Pauline stood up. "I'm afraid I can't discuss this any longer." She held out a muscled hand. Manisha stared at it for a moment, and then stood and grasped Pauline's palm briefly.

"I'm sorry," Pauline said again. She stepped away from the table and held open the door. Manisha turned and walked out.

Pauline's secretary Jessica, in the alcove, had her eyes trained on her computer screen. Jessica did not greet Manisha or look at her as she walked past.

Manisha strode through the empty hallway, clutching the manila folders to her chest. She squeezed her eyes shut. One tear slid down her cheek.

*

"I can't tell my mother," Manisha said.

"She'll be worried," Lee Ann agreed.

They walked along a sidewalk next to a development of new condos. Lee Ann's renovated farmhouse was visible in the distance behind them. The roadway was lined with thin saplings just leafing out.

"She'll think I'm a failure. As usual." Manisha pumped her arms and swung her legs over the new white sidewalk. Her open coat flared behind her.

"Manisha, she doesn't think you're a failure!" Lee Ann

clutched her arms around her pink fleece jacket, trotting to keep up with her friend.

"I didn't become a doctor, like she wanted me to. I got a PhD but couldn't get a tenure-track job." Manisha spat out each sentence between breaths. "Then I thought I'd do something different. I told her I was going to be a role model for all those kids. Instead, I get kicked out because someone complained that I don't have a teaching license."

Lee Ann jogged a few steps to catch up. "Have you spoken to the human resources department about this? It seems unfair to let you go because you don't have a license, when they knew—"

"There is no human resources department. Pauline handles all the hiring, all the evaluations. She decides who gets a contract and who doesn't."

An old basset hound strolled past, leading a young man thumbing his phone screen.

"Have you contacted the university about getting your old job back?"

"I sent an e-mail to my department head. I'm sure I can get something part-time at least."

"And you can get back on Gerard's insurance."

"Eventually, I'll have to tell my mother, and my kids. And Gerard. They'll all think I'm a failure."

"You're not a failure, Manisha!"

"I can't even keep a job teaching eleven-year-olds."

*

Manisha was dreaming. She walked down the school hallway which swarmed with young bodies. Voices bounced off the walls and lockers clanged. She threaded her way through the crowd, hurrying to get somewhere.

Someone—a young clean-cut man whom she didn't recognize—walked up to her and handed her a large cardboard vat. She grasped it in both outstretched arms, and the man hurried away. It was heavy. She could just see into the partially open top. It was filled with dirty, scummy water. Dirty toilet water.

As she walked, she realized what she was carrying: a milk carton, a giant version of the waxed-cardboard half-pint containers the kids drank from at lunch. The dirty water sloshed around. She could see bits of toilet paper and scum and maybe solid matter. She didn't want to look. She knew she had to carry it without spilling it, and without letting the kids see inside. She wasn't sure where she was going, or what she was supposed to do with this vat of dirty water, but she knew this was her responsibility now.

APRIL

Saturday morning. Manisha startled out of sleep. She sat up in her dark bedroom, eyes wide. The doorbell rang, followed by banging on the door. The red numbers of her clock showed 5:48.

Manisha threw aside her covers, switched on her bedside lamp, and wrapped a terry robe around herself. She flicked on the light in the hallway and squinted into each child's room. Both were in bed, asleep.

The doorbell rang again. Clutching her robe around her, Manisha descended the stairs. Her heart raced. She pushed aside the living room curtains and saw a black and white police car in the driveway. The sky was still dim. When she unlocked and opened the door, a cold wind rushed into the house, puddling around her bare ankles and feet, reaching for her throat.

Two police officers stood on the porch: a tall, thin white man, and a tall, thin African-American woman. The breeze tugged at their navy-blue open coats. The woman held a large manila envelope. The man had his hands clasped in front of him. Both wore somber expressions.

"Good morning, ma'am. We're looking for Manisha Venkataraman," the woman said, pronouncing the syllables carefully.

"I am Manisha."

"I'm Officer Renee Cowan." She held out a hand, which Manisha shook.

"Officer Mike Holder." The male officer reached out his hand.

"Ma'am, we have some bad news, I'm afraid," the woman said.

"What is it? My husband?"

"May we come in?"

Manisha opened the door wider. Her blood throbbed in her neck and head. She stepped aside as the officers entered. They waited while she shut out the wind.

"We'd like to sit down," the woman said, and Manisha led them to the living room. Once they were all seated, Officer Cowan began speaking.

"An hour ago, we received an anonymous phone call. It concerned a woman named Bhagya Venkataraman."

"My mother!" Manisha gasped. "Is she OK?"

"The caller gave us an address. When we arrived, we found her lying on the sofa. We could not find a pulse. We called an ambulance, and started CPR, but nothing could be done."

Manisha stared. "But . . . I just saw her a few days ago. She seemed fine."

"Ma'am, it appeared to be a suicide. An empty bottle of prescription painkillers was found on the table next to her. She left a letter for the police, and this for you." The officer now held out the envelope.

Manisha reached for it. She glanced wide-eyed from her name, printed in an unfamiliar handwriting, to the officers' faces. The envelope was not sealed. With trembling hands, she pushed aside the flap and removed several items: a hand-written letter on yellow legal-pad paper; a typed letter; a list of names and addresses; a typed document entitled "Last Will and Testament;" and a printed form, filled in with neat blue pen, with the heading "Donor Registration Form, Willed Body Program." The yellow letter was in her mother's familiar Indian-style cursive, the writing shaky in places. Several letters and words had been gone over twice, painstakingly, with the pen.

My Dear Manisha,

I asked the police to give this to you. By now you must have heard the news. I am afraid it is shocking.

I have made a decision to do something you might not approve of. I did not want to wait too long. Already I am forgetting so much. My short-term memory is not good. My handwriting is deteror not good.

I hope you will understand why I have chosen this way to end my life. When I told you about my disease, you said you would take care of me. I thank you very much. I did not want to leave you that burden.

I am so very sorry to have to leave you in this way. I do not want to live without my mind. I do not want to live without knowing who I am or how I am conducting myself.

You have given me the gift of motherhood, and I did not appreciate it fully. I have not been a good mother to you. I wanted you to be someone you are not. I hope you can forgive me.

I do not want a funeral. I have made arrangements with a

*medical school to take my body. The police have been in-
formed of this. I do not believe in spending money on a dead
body.*

*Manisha, my will is in order. I have included a list of
bank accounts, as well as contact information for my lawyer
and accountant. You and the children will be taken care of
financially.*

I hope you can understand this last decision of mine.

*With all my love,
Bhagya Venkataraman, M.D.*

Manisha folded the paper and tried to stuff everything
back into the envelope. The papers would not go in. She tossed
everything onto the sofa cushion. "Are you sure it was . . ."
Manisha couldn't get the words out. "You said someone called
you. Who was it?"

"We have no way of knowing," the woman answered. "The
call came from a pay phone at the airport."

"Can you collect fingerprints in the house?"

"We have someone dusting for fingerprints. We will investigate. But the note your mother left for the police made it very
clear that she intended to do what she did."

"I need to go to her."

"We're ready when you are. We'll follow you there. We do
want to let you know that there are police officers still at the
scene, as well as the coroner."

Manisha stood. "Nat?" She ran up the stairs. "Nat!" He
was face-down on his bed. She shook him awake. "I need your
help right now. I have to go to grandma's house. It's an emer-
gency. When Charlotte wakes up, help her with whatever she
needs. Breakfast, or whatever. Call me on my cell when you're

both awake and dressed."

Nat bolted up and nodded.

"OK. Go back to sleep now." She patted him as he lowered himself to the mattress, eyes wide and bewildered.

*

As she drove to her mother's condo, a low table of clouds hung in the sky. Dark branches, some still bare of leaves, whipped in the wind. She turned into the driveway of the condo development and passed the pods of white houses with brown trim. Each tiny yard was planted with a new tree in the same location. Each house foundation was lined with the same bushes. Except for the numbers, they all looked alike.

Two other vehicles occupied the parking spaces in front of her mother's condo: a police car, and a van painted with the words "Coroner." She slid into the neighbor's parking place. The police car following pulled up beside her.

The garage door was open. Besides her mother's car, the only other items on the clean floor of the garage were a large wheeled trash can, an empty recycling bin, and a snow shovel.

The door from the garage into the house was unlocked, and the officers motioned for Manisha to step in first. Inside, the air was cool and smelled of spices, as usual. The officers strode past her as Manisha kicked off her shoes. Unfamiliar people milled around the living room, their voices echoing from the bare walls.

Manisha crept forward and set her purse on the counter near the stove. Every possible light had been turned on: the kitchen was ablaze, and the living room lamp glared. Someone was taking pictures with a phone camera. A crowd of people surrounded the sofa, which was in an odd position. Manisha was looking at the back of the couch. It had been moved to face the sliding glass doors. The curtains were wide open. She approached, and the crowd made way for her. A figure lay on the sofa under a cloth, bathed by the cold morning light. Manisha rushed towards it and knelt on the floor. She lifted her hand to the cloth, but stopped in mid-air. Her eyes rested on a black and silver boombox on the floor, from which came soft music: a sitar, and a woman's soft, high voice. She looked around her. Officer Cowan came forward and pulled the shroud back from the face.

Her mother's eyes were closed, the corners of her mouth turned down. Manisha hovered her hand above the forehead, and then, without touching the figure on the sofa, she stood up. The boombox's two black speakers were large, staring eyes.

"Do you want to call a friend or family member to be with you?" the police officer asked.

Manisha looked back at the counter where her purse sat. "What happens next?" she whispered.

"The coroner will take the body in for an autopsy. We'll need to gather more information from you about your mother's medical history and mental health."

Manisha sank to the floor again and rested her forehead on the sofa, inches from her mother's ear.

*

Monday evening. Manisha stood in a small office facing Lyle, Lee Ann's husband, who sat behind a wood desk strewn with newspapers, typed manuscript pages, and reference books. The walls around them displayed framed posters of historic front pages of the newspaper for which Lyle worked as an editor. Through the picture window opposite the door was a view of a bridge, its concrete arches marching across the river.

From her leather shoulder bag Manisha withdrew a creased

sheet of paper, which she placed onto the desk. "Lyle." She cleared her throat. "When I was looking through the envelope my mother left for me, I found this letter."

Lyle stood and approached her from behind the desk. "Manisha. I'm so sorry. We're here for you."

"Thank you, Lyle. Lee Ann's already helped so much. But right now—please, look at this letter."

He pulled an extra chair around to his side of the desk, and once she was seated, he perched on his own wheeled chair. He glanced at the letter. His eyes did not travel back and forth over the lines of type. Instead, they stared at the signature at the bottom.

Dear Editor,

I would like to use this forum to thank the community, which welcomed me more than 30 years ago when I became the first woman surgeon at Lincoln County Hospital. Even though I am an immigrant, still you made me feel part of this community, and I was proud to become a US citizen at the earliest opportunity.

As an obstetrician and gynecologist, I have been blessed to deliver many babies who have grown up to be productive, valued members of the community. I was also glad to introduce new approaches such as natural childbirth and alternatives to hysterectomy.

Recently, I have been accused of introducing a controversial approach: doctor-assisted suicide for those with terminal or incurable illness as an alternative to living with intense pain, fear, or suffering.

Some months ago, one of my patients came in with her mother. The old woman had breast cancer which had

*metastasized into her bones. She had already had surgery,
radiation, chemotherapy. Everything that could be done, had
already been done. The woman was in severe pain. In fact,
she moaned continuously in my office. Her own doctor refused
to prescribe more medication, because this woman had such
a tolerance to morphine that a higher dose was likely to kill
her. The daughter was living with her mother, taking care
of her. She could see how her mother suffered. I examined the
mother and considered her request. And I wrote a prescription. The mother died the same night.*

*The new medical director at the hospital believes that I did
not fully comprehend the consequences of my actions. But I
knew exactly what I was doing. I acted alone. My colleagues
and supervisors at the hospital knew nothing about this, nor
should they be held accountable for what is, unfortunately,
still considered illegal in most of the country.*

*By the time you read this, I will have, by my own hand,
taken my life. I was diagnosed with Alzheimer's which, as
most of you know, is incurable. I have chosen what I believe
to be an honorable way to end my life, so as to inflict the least
amount of suffering on my colleagues, friends, relatives, and
myself.*

*I hope that soon my choice will be legally available to every
human being who would like control of this final life decision.*

Sincerely,
Bhagya Venkataraman, M.D.

While the letter had been typed flawlessly, the signature
seemed scribbled by a child's hand.

"Did she send this to you?" Manisha asked. She clutched
the leather shoulder bag in her lap.

"I received it this morning. I've read it many times. We've talked about it at our editors' meeting."

"And? Will you publish it?"

"We'll definitely do a short article about her life. And her death. We'll have to mention the controversy surrounding her at the hospital."

"But what about publishing her letter?"

Lyle shook his head. "I'm afraid the answer is no."

"Why not?"

"Unfortunately, the paper is not a forum for personal messages. I did explain that to your mother."

"She talked to you about it?"

"At Thanksgiving, she asked me how to get a letter published in the newspaper."

Manisha wilted over her bag. "I didn't know." She rapped herself on the head. "I didn't want to know. She even tried to ask for my help." Manisha covered her face with her hands. "She planned this for spring break, Lyle, so I'd have time to deal with it. Even in death, she was considerate of me." She remained motionless.

Lyle folded the letter. She followed his gaze to the view outside. Along the river, the windows of gray downtown skyscrapers glimmered in the dusk.

MAY

Manisha squatted at the shelf behind her desk, dropping books into two paper grocery sacks. On the desk, surrounding the laptop, were small gift bags, square white card envelopes, a clear plastic box of cookies, and a potted African violet, its fuzzy leaves crowned with magenta flowers. The gift tags and envelopes bore the names of her students: Aliya, Kay, Wilson, Izzie.

Outside the classroom windows the bright light of day was fading.

A knock on the door. Donna entered and walked forward with her arms outstretched. Manisha stood and stepped into the hug.

"I'm sorry for not asking you about your plans," Donna murmured. "I haven't known what to say."

"We'll stay in touch," Manisha said.

"You have made a difference this year. I want you to know that."

Manisha touched the inside of her eye with a fingertip. "Thank you."

"If you need any help . . . a recommendation . . . anything, just contact me."

"Thank you, Donna. I'll let you know what happens."

"Please do. Can I carry something for you?"

Manisha looked down at the grocery sacks. "I think I want to do this by myself."

"I understand." Donna stepped back. "Bye, then." She gave a little wave, and was out the door.

Manisha placed the children's gifts into a sack. She glanced at the bookshelf and peeked under the desk. The room was empty and clean. Holding both bags, she walked out of the room for the last time. She avoided the main hallway, which went past Pauline's office, and instead exited the side door of the school.

Outside, she was startled to see Jessica, Pauline's assistant, striding to the parking lot from the main doorway. Manisha kept her eyes away from Jessica as they both made their way to their cars, but it was soon apparent that their paths would cross.

Jessica stopped abruptly. Her leopard print tote hung from one arm.

"Goodbye," Manisha said as she approached, weighed down with her grocery sacks.

"Manisha. I would like to say something to you." Jessica's face was serious, almost stern. She clutched her keys in her fist.

Manisha stopped.

Jessica squinted in the sunlight. "Do you have any idea why you didn't receive another contract?" Her voice was muted, although no one else was nearby.

"Well, I decided that . . . this job was not quite right for me."

"I know what really happened. I can hear everything that goes on in Pauline's office."

"It's my license. Or lack thereof. I've decided to—"

"It has nothing to do with your license."

"Some parents complained."

"One particular family complained. After Grandparents' Day."

Manisha set down the heavy bags. "It was the skits, wasn't it?"

"This family claims that you tried to introduce your religion to the students, and—"

"What religion?"

Jessica touched her forehead. "Isn't it the Hindus who wear the dot?"

Manisha stared at her. "Who was it?"

"I don't want to . . . I wasn't going to tell you at all, but when I saw you with all your stuff . . ." Jessica transferred her knot of keys to her other hand. "I want you to know that this has nothing to do with your teaching, and everything to do with money."

"Was it Izzie's family?"

Jessica stepped away, towards her own minivan.

"Are you sure you heard correctly?" Manisha picked up her

bags and followed.

"You think I'm making this up?"

"I just . . . it's hard for me to believe that Pauline would get rid of a good teacher for . . . Pauline's not like that. She's committed to diversity."

"You can believe whatever you want." Jessica's car beeped as she opened the driver's side door, tossed her bag across to the passenger seat, and got behind the wheel.

"It was Wilson's family, wasn't it?"

"Does it matter?" Jessica slammed the car door shut. Manisha stepped away and watched as she started the vehicle, backed out, and drove away.

*

Lee Ann and Manisha walked along a path in a park, past a huge flowering wisteria spilling over a brick wall. The sun shone through wispy clouds overhead.

Manisha wore a faded pair of jeans and beat-up leather shoes. "I've been reading Mom's journal. Lee Ann, I just can't believe she had Alzheimer's. Her memory seems fine."

"Old memories are different from recent memories," Lee Ann reminded her.

Their footsteps crunched over the bark-strewn path. A breeze rustled the leaves of the trees around them.

"I keep wondering who helped her." Manisha's voice was a low monotone. "Someone drove her to Indianapolis. Someone addressed those envelopes for her. Someone filled out those forms for her. Someone helped her write that letter to the editor."

"I think it might have been a nurse who used to work with her."

"Marisol?"

"Someone from years ago. Olga."

Manisha stopped and frowned at Lee Ann. "How do you know?"

"This is what I've been hearing at work."

"Why didn't you tell me?"

"I wasn't sure how much you wanted to know."

Manisha shifted her gaze to the row of trees behind Lee Ann. Through them, shining in the distance, appeared a small pond fringed with reeds. "Olga. I should've guessed. Mom had her over for dinner, and . . ." Manisha raised her hand to her throat. "Lee Ann, I feel like I hardly knew my mother. Is there anything else you've heard?"

"Nothing else. But I do want to say that if it was Olga, then your mom was in good hands. Olga is one of the most—"

"I don't want to know." Manisha began walking again.

"OK."

"Mom said she wanted my help. But when I went over there, she wouldn't tell me what really happened. She didn't trust me. She didn't think I'd understand. But she trusted Olga."

"She might not have wanted to burden you."

"I wonder if Mom suspected that I'd need financial help." Manisha watched her shoes step along the path. "I never told Mom that I lost the job, but I wonder if she knew this would happen, and if she did what she did just so I'd have—"

"No." Lee Ann stopped. Her voice was stern. She put her hands on Manisha's shoulders. "Don't even think that. Manisha, I know people who worked with your mom. From what they said about her performance right before she retired, I really do believe that she was in the early stages of dementia. I think she knew exactly what was going on with her health."

Manisha was sobbing. Lee Ann put her arms around her friend and hugged her tight. "Do you want to sit down?" she murmured. "There's a bench up ahead."

"It helps to keep moving." Manisha removed a pack of tissues from her jeans pocket and wiped her face. They had reached the pond and stopped to watch the ducks floating by, the mottled brown mama leading a row of ducklings. "I didn't tell you yet, Lee Ann, but I was offered a full-time job at the university."

"And?"

"I start next week."

Lee Ann rubbed her friend's back. "They're lucky to have you. But don't you want to take the summer off to spend time with the kids?"

"They'll be away with Gerard in July. Charlotte has already picked out way too many summer camps, and Nat'll hang out at his best friend's house."

"Is it a teaching job?"

"I'll be doing writing, editing, and administrative work at the business school. I'll basically be a glorified secretary. I'm glad my mom didn't have to see this. But here's the thing—I'll get paid more than what I made as an adjunct, I'll get benefits, and I can take free classes towards my teaching license."

"So, you still want to be a teacher."

"I really did love working with the kids. At the end of the year, a lot of them knew I wasn't coming back, and they wrote the sweetest cards to me. Even Wilson and Izzie."

"And their parents are the ones . . ."

"I'm not sure." Manisha shook her head. "I have no idea, really. Even after what Jessica said, I wonder if . . . I just wasn't a good enough teacher. I wonder if Pauline was right about that." Manisha's head descended.

"She was happy with you before."

"She seemed to be." Manisha took a long breath. "My first-period students chose that story for their skit. I keep thinking, if only I had told them to pick a different scene, then maybe . . ."

"Maybe you'd still be at a school that discriminates against minority teachers?"

"I guess . . . it's better to know the truth."

Lee Ann tucked a lock of hair behind her ear. "You're moving on to better things."

"Next time I get a teaching job, I'll stick with the textbook. I won't do anything that draws attention to my ethnicity."

"That's too bad," Lee Ann said. "I'm sure you'll be a great teacher no matter what, but the kids won't be able to benefit from your unique life experience."

"My unique life experience isn't going to help me keep a job as a teacher."

*

On the bow windowsill behind Manisha's desk, amidst the etched candle holder and potted African violet, stood Bhagya's gold medal in a wooden coin holder.

Her computer screen displayed the US government seal: an eagle with outstretched wings clutching arrows in one clawed foot, and an olive branch in the other. Next to this seal were the words "Equal Employment Opportunity Commission." Manisha's eyes traveled along the paragraph below the seal, which read:

> The U.S. Equal Employment Opportunity Commission (EEOC) is responsible for enforcing federal laws that make it illegal to discriminate against a job applicant or an employee because of the person's race, color, religion, sex (including pregnancy), national origin, age (40 or older), disability or genetic information.

She clicked on a link: Filing a Charge.

JUNE

"Manisha Venkataraman," a woman's voice said, repeating the name slowly. "Am I pronouncing it correctly?"

"Close enough." Manisha sat in the driver's seat of her car with her cell phone pressed to her ear. The air conditioner blew chilly air at her. She was in the parking lot of a wide brick building, its central tower flanked by two glassed-in corridors. The sun glared down from directly overhead. Students in jeans and backpacks streamed over the grassy commons on either side.

The car seat had been pushed all the way back, and on Manisha's lap lay a typed document attached to a clipboard. In the top margin of this document she had written the name "Alma Garcia," and she traced these letters with her pen.

"As you know, I'm one of the lawyers assigned to your region." Alma Garcia's Midwestern accent was slow and firm. "I have your file here. I see that you are claiming religious discrimination."

"Yes."

"What religion are you?"

"I—well, my mother was raised Hindu. But we didn't follow that at home. I guess I don't really have a religion."

"Are you an atheist, then?"

"I wouldn't go that far. Religion isn't something I think about much."

"According to EEOC guidelines, in order to claim religious discrimination, you must have been treated unfairly because of your religion."

"They thought I had a religion. I was fired because of what other people assumed about me and my religion." The name in the top margin had acquired a box around it. Manisha traced over the borders of the box.

Alma cleared her throat. "If you don't have a religion, then I'm afraid that what happened to you doesn't fit into our guidelines for religious discrimination."

Manisha stopped tracing. "Oh."

"That category is for people who have been denied accommodation based on religious belief, or who have been harassed because of their religion. You aren't claiming harassment."

"Isn't it harassment to be fired unjustly?"

"Harassment is when someone makes repeated, offensive remarks about your religion. Did that happen to you?"

"It was all a secret. So, no. But if you investigate, you might find other instances of discrimination. I'm sure this is not the first time something like this has happened at this school."

"We don't investigate employers without evidence first."

"I see."

"I don't think there is anything I can do for you," Alma Garcia said.

"Oh." Manisha drew parallel lines through the "A" of the name. "Well. Thank you."

"You have a good day now."

"You too."

"Goodbye."

Manisha pulled the phone from her ear and ended the call. She stacked the phone on the clipboard and set both on the passenger seat. Her blue gemstone ring winked in the sunlight. She leaned forward until her forehead was supported by the steering wheel. The cold air from the vents chilled her ears.

*

Sitting cross-legged in the center of her unmade bed, Manisha held her mother's yellow legal pad on her lap. The bedside lamp cast a glow over the bed, but the rest of the room lay in dimness.

She turned past her mother's handwriting to a blank sheet near the back. She bit her lip and forced the pen tip to the page.

Dear Mom,

I wish you were here. I wish we could talk again the way we did during my birthday dinner. I wish I could listen to you with truly open ears.

You told me that other people misunderstood you, and that's why you were trying to write the story of your life. Even your own daughter didn't take the time to understand you. I'm so sorry, Mom. I lost my chance to get to know you when you were still here with me.

Mom, now that I've read what you've written, I can see how you struggled. Despite the discrimination you faced, you believed you had better opportunities in this country, and you wanted me to benefit from those opportunities. I have not done what you envisioned. I did not stand on your shoulders and reach higher. I did not fulfil your hopes. I spent years rebelling against what I thought you wanted me to be. I've made a mess of my life.

I have failed at so many things. I lost my job. I have no marriage. Even the EEOC says I have no case. In some ways I feel like an idiot about what happened at work. Donna tried to warn me. I should have been more careful. I should have recognized that people are conservative when it comes to their children.

Manisha curled up still clutching the legal pad. Tears dripped down the side of her face. She used the bedsheet to wipe them away. A lone car whooshed by on the street.

She pushed herself up, grabbed a tissue from the nightstand and blew her nose. Then, putting pen to paper again, she wrote:

> *I've lost a lot, but I have gained one thing. I have your love. I had it all along, but I did not know it.*

*

Saturday morning. Manisha and Lee Ann worked in Manisha's kitchen as clear sunshine washed the room.

"How did it go with Gerard yesterday?" Lee Ann, her hair in a bandana, wiped the etched glass candleholder with a damp towel.

"We signed." Manisha balanced on a stepstool, pulling dusty vases out of a high cupboard and lowering them to the counter.

"You agreed on everything?"

Manisha stepped down. "I'll stay in the house. He'll pay child support. He offered more than I asked for. I think he feels guilty."

"He should." Lee Ann held up the candle holder. "What're you going to do with this? It has your name and his name on it."

Manisha took the item into her own hands and considered the etched inscription. "I'm going to break it."

"You're not!"

"I can give away our other wedding presents, but who would want this?" She strode out the back door onto the deck.

Lee Ann followed, shaking her head. "Good thing the kids aren't home to see this."

Hanging from trees nearby were two bird feeders: a tube of seeds, and a red and yellow platform supporting a clear container full of sugar syrup.

Manisha ran her finger over the silver edging of the glass. Then she lifted the object to a horizontal position above her head. "Here it goes."

Lee Ann crossed her arms and watched as the wedding gift left Manisha's hand and met the wooden deck floor. It cracked into three pieces.

"At least it didn't make too much of a mess." Manisha poked her sneakered toe at the shattered glass. She attempted a laugh. Her chin puckered, and Lee Ann reached over the destruction to gather her friend into her arms.

*

After dinner, Manisha drove out alone, past the neighborhood where she had grown up, and parked by a path near the creek.

Faint ripples of clouds decorated the northern part of the sky. A large bird—a hawk, maybe—soared above. The wings were scalloped along the fringed edges. It skimmed high above her across the air, a trim torpedo body, a fan of tail feathers, and dark, outstretched wings against the deep blue sky.

She gasped, heart pounding in her throat. She dropped her eyes to steady herself, nailing her sight to the gray pavement at her feet. Her rhythms slowed, and she allowed her gaze to drift out, to the gurgling stream beside the path, and into the dark woods.

She inched her eyes up to the vast blueness again. The hawk hung in the sky. Her heart trembling in her neck, she whispered aloud the lines of a poem by William Butler Yeats:

I will not be clapped in a hood,
Nor a cage, nor alight upon wrist,
Now I have learnt to be proud
Hovering over the wood
In the broken mist
Or tumbling cloud.

She recited the poem over and over, head tipped back,
watching the hawk soaring, beckoning like a big hand.

acknowledgements

Thank you so much to Minerva Rising Press for selecting this collection as the winner of their Rosemary Daniell fiction contest. It has been absolutely wonderful working with founder and editor Kim Brown, whose suggestions were wise and insightful. Chelsey Clammer, copy editor, did careful and thorough work. For the beautiful, striking cover, I thank Lauren Chidel and Brooke Schultz, and for a crisp, clear interior, I thank Brooke Schultz.

The novella *Hawk* had its origin in a longer novel, which was a finalist for the 2014 Bellwether Prize for Socially Engaged Fiction. Many people helped with the genesis and revision of that novel and this novella. I interviewed the following women doctors of Indian origin: Dr. Pushpa Bathija, Dr. Sheela Kashkari, and the late Dr. Leela Swamy. I thank them for their time and their insights. I also interviewed my father, Dr. V. V. Sreenivasan, about his experiences as an immigrant doctor. Several people critiqued drafts of the novel and novella: Kathy Beckwith, Sindya Bhanoo, Herta Feely, Jenni Ferrari-Adler, Laraine Herring, Cyndi Pauwels, Merryl Winstein, and Sarah Winstein-Hibbs. Thank you all for your suggestions.

In the process of revising my short fiction, I benefited from writing groups, writing friends, and unmet people who critiqued my stories online via the Zoetrope Virtual Studio. Please know that your careful reading and perceptive comments were invaluable to me. Thank you as well to my parents, Vimala and V.V. Sreenivasan, who not only commented on the stories, but have always supported my writing.

I would also like to thank the Washington, DC Commission on the Arts and Humanities for two grants. The Sewanee Writers' Conference, the Taos Writers Conference, and the

Antioch Writers' Workshop allowed me to I benefit from the ideas, support, and fellowship of other writers.

The following stories have been previously published in slightly different form: "Mirror," anthologized in *Mamas and Papas: On the Sublime and Heartbreaking Art of Parenting*, Sunbelt Publications, 2010, and published in *Green Hills Literary Lantern*, Truman State University, Kirksville, MO, summer 2005; "At Home" (original title: "Home"), *The Drum Literary Magazine*, April 2012; "Revolution," *Sixfold*, Winter 2015; "Dreams," *Phantasmagoria*, White Bear Lake, MN, summer 2005; "The Sweater," *Bellowing Ark*, Shoreline, WA, July/August 2010; "Mrs. Raghavendra's Daughter," *Catamaran*, University of Connecticut, volume 5, 2006; "Crystal Vase: Snapshots," *Copper Nickel*, University of Colorado-Denver, fall 2018; "Perfect Sunday," *India Currents*, San Jose, CA, January 2012. Thank you so much to the editors of these magazines.

about the author

Author photo by Aline Yamada

Jyotsna Sreenivasan was born and raised in Ohio. Her parents are immigrants from India. She is the author of the novel *And Laughter Fell From the Sky*. Her short stories have been published in literary magazines and anthologies. She was a finalist for the 2014 PEN Bellwether Prize for Socially Engaged Fiction and received an Artist Fellowship Grant from the Washington, DC Commission on the Arts. *These Americans* is her first short story collection. For information about Jyotsna as well as other writers who are children of immigrants, please see

www.SecondGenStories.com.

CPSIA information can be obtained
at www.ICGtesting.com
Printed in the USA
LVHW030012230821
695874LV00002B/196